To Flo
Happy
and ...
x Hi~ x
x

HELL UNEARTHED

A Modern Adaptation of Dante's Inferno

HILARY McELWAINE

THE CHOIR PRESS

Contents

To my mother, whose faith lay in humanity, and to my father, whose unwavering faith was with God.

"Quali fioretti, dal notturno gelo
chinati e chiusi, poi che 'l sol li 'imbianca
si drizzan tutti aperti in loro stelo:"

Inferno, Canto II vv 127-129

Like little flowers that,
tightly shut and curled in on themselves in the night's chill,
unfurl their petals and straighten up tall when the morning sun warms them:

"… seggendo in piuma,
in fama non si vien, né sotto coltre;
sanza la qual chi sua vita consuma,
cotal vestigio in terra di sé lascia,
qual fummo in aere e in acqua la schiuma.
E però leva sú: vinci l'ambascia
con l'animo che vince ogne battaglia,
se col suo grave corpo non s'accascia."

Inferno, canto XXIV vv 47-54

It takes hard work and dedication to achieve progress and happiness
and leave your mark in life.
If you sit on a bed of feathers or hide under your duvet,
you will leave nothing of note on this earth.
Your life will be forgotten like a puff of smoke.

Foreword

Dante completed the *Divine Comedy* 700 years ago in 1320 then died the following year. It is one of the greatest works of literature of all time. As TS Eliot said, "Dante and Shakespeare divide the world between them. There is no third."

For such a rich and enthralling work to be the preserve mainly of academics is wrong. I was fortunate to be introduced to Dante's masterpiece at the age of sixteen and having spent years at school, university and beyond being inspired by his writing, I am keen to pass on my enjoyment to others. My objective with this adaptation is to bring Dante to a wider readership of both young adults and adults who will be entertained by the breadth and colour of its characters, drawn from biblical, classical, contemporary and modern sources, and the eternal fascination with life after death.

The *Divine Comedy* has inspired a number of works of literature over the years, including James Joyce's epic novel *Ulysses*, Tolkein's *Lord of the Rings* and Lewis Carroll's *Alice in Wonderland*. It has also captured the imagination of visual artists like Auguste Rodin with his sculpture of the *Gates of Hell* and William Blake's *Divine Comedy Illustrations*. Most recently, the *Divine Comedy* has supported the narrative arc of TV shows like *Mad Men* and the video game *Dante's Inferno*. Even *Game of Thrones* with its fusion of medieval history and mythical fantasy clearly draws on the *Divine Comedy*.

Inferno (Hell) is the first part of the *Divine Comedy* where Dante journeys through the underworld meeting a cast of sinners. They are positioned in Hell according to the gravity of their sin and tormented by fire, boiling blood, sticky tar or ice. Some are stuck headfirst in holes with their legs wiggling about in the air; others are clawed or hooked by demons.

The subject matter is intriguing precisely because no one is able to come back and tell of their experience after death. Do we really suffer for our wrongdoings after we have died? What is happiness? What is it to achieve greatness in life, and how is that greatness viewed in the afterlife? How should we live our lives to ensure happiness or salvation after we die? What makes society and local communities strong? Dante's answers to these questions are timeless: they make as much sense then as now. To prove the point, I have woven in stories of crime and immorality from the modern day – and from across countries, religions and cultures – and they are aligned with Dante's original messages. I have shaken up Hell to include modern day sins and have reordered them within a framework of criminal law as we know it today. I have remained faithful to Dante's overarching Aristotelian structure, with its three categories of Self-indulgence, Violence and Fraud. I have chosen stories, both fictional and true, from the modern day and from history, and I have placed them alongside a meaningful selection of the classical stories, biblical stories and contemporary history as retold by Dante. The message remains the same. Happiness is achieved through peace and stability in government with clear moral guidance coming from a spiritual power. What we achieve in life, and how, will ultimately be judged by God.

The defining style of the *Divine Comedy* is Dante's decision to write in the vernacular of his local Tuscan language. Almost all works of high literature up to this point were written in Latin, the language of the literati and the signifier of upbringing, class and knowledge. Dante was happy without those signifiers and for his words to speak for themselves. He wanted his epic to reach a wide audience and not just a narrow elite and to do that he needed to write it in the language of the people. Dante explained this choice to his leading patron, an important nobleman called Can Grande della Scala, as driven by a desire to make it easy to read, humble in tone and specifically inclusive of people, both men and women, who didn't have access to a Latin education.

With *Hell Unearthed*, I have taken Dante's mission further, to bring *Inferno* to people who may be interested in reading it for the pure enjoyment of the story and appreciation of its messages rather than as a vehicle for academic study. You don't have to be an art expert to enjoy works of art, and the same should be true for works of literature in whatever language they originate.

Hell Unearthed offers a new and modernised reading experience and still conveys the themes espoused by Dante. There is an index of noteworthy characters where extra explanations or a quick reminder of a character's background will enhance the reading experience or satisfy a thirst for knowledge. As a highly visual piece of writing, my adaptation includes modern illustrations to accompany each canto aiming to shine a light on the characters, punishments and topography of Hell to support the reading experience.

Writing this at the time of the Covid-19 pandemic resonates with Dante's exile from his native city, Florence, during which time Dante produced the *Divine Comedy*. The sense of being shut out from normal, familiar life perhaps makes us focus more on the things we really care about. Out of these tragedies, good things, indeed comedies, can come.

Introduction

Dante's Divine Comedy

Dante entitled his trilogy of Hell, Purgatory and Paradise *"La Commedia"* (the Comedy) as most epic works of literature were classified as either Comedy or Tragedy, the distinction being whether there was a happy ending or not. In the 1370s, fifty years after Dante's death, Boccaccio was commissioned by the city of Florence to deliver lectures on Dante to the general public, making Dante the first contemporary author to gain a place alongside the ancient classics on university courses. The story's Christian allegory of Man seeking atonement for his sins and then reaching redemption through Purgatory resulted, several years after the author's death, in the addition of "Divina" to the title, and so it became the *Divine Comedy*.

The *Divine Comedy* is set within a framework of medieval Christian belief, but the characters Dante includes come from a wide range of occupations, eras and geographies. There are philosophers, writers, popes, politicians, teachers, military leaders, church leaders, as well as biblical and fictional characters. These characters reflect the breadth of influences on life in Italy at the time Dante was alive. Immigration and migration from central Europe and the East had resulted in the spread of foreign arts, literature and ideas, all of which are celebrated in the *Divine Comedy*.

The work is made up of three parts or canticles: Hell, Purgatory and Paradise. Each canticle contains 33 cantos with Hell having an extra introductory canto to give 100 cantos in total. There are 9 circles in Hell, 9 steps of Purgatory and 9 heavens in Paradise. The sets of 3 and 9 relate to the Holy Trinity of God the Father, the Son and the Holy Ghost. The mathematical structure of the original poem and its rhyming scheme provide a scientific physical framework which contrasts with the divine nature of Dante's journey through Hell, Purgatory and Paradise.

The journey through each of these worlds takes place at Easter in 1300. Dante is 35 at the start of his journey. The number is significant because it is half of the biblical lifespan of 70 and he is therefore at life's mid-point. He feels insecure at the passage of time, uncertain of his future and anxious about how he might find the right "way" to make it to Heaven, his ultimate aspirational destination. Today we might describe this state of mind as a mid-life crisis. For Dante, there are certainly moral overtones as he feels lost in the darkness of life's sins and hopes to cleanse himself of past wrongdoings and be worthy of a place in the purity of Paradise. The journey starts on Maundy Thursday recalling when Jesus held the last supper with his disciples before his crucifixion, and ends on Easter Sunday, linking Dante's arrival at the gates of Heaven with the resurrection and representing the soul's reconciliation with God.

Dante chooses the classical poet, Virgil, as his guide through the underworld. His choice reflects the enormous admiration he had for classical literature and also draws a parallel between Dante and Aeneas who were both forced from their native cities, Dante as an exile, Aeneas fleeing Troy as it was razed by the Greeks. In the early part of Purgatory, Virgil hands Dante over to Beatrice who represents happiness and divine revelation and who guides him onwards towards Paradise. Virgil's usefulness as a guide is limited as he is a Pagan who lived before Christ and is therefore deprived of the knowledge of salvation. Beatrice's character is based on a young acquaintance called Bici Portinari whom Dante idealised into a symbol of beauty, purity, and grace, culminating in her role as Dante's guide to Paradise.

Political and historical background

At the beginning of the 13th Century, Italy was a bundle of independent city republics with no formal centre of government – a far cry from the cohesive nature of the Roman Empire. There was constant feuding and rivalry between cities, between aristocrats and the labouring classes and also between different noble families with their tribal jealousies.

Central Italy was politically divided between Guelphs and Ghibellines. While it is common today for opposing political parties to co-exist relatively peacefully, in Medieval Italy, opposing political views often became violent and warring families would take the law into their own hands. Picture Shakespeare's Romeo and Juliet with the fighting Montague and Capulet families who supported the Ghibellines and Guelphs respectively. Despite significant economic success through trade in silks, dyes and spices procured from the East, politically things were unravelling, and warring parties were prepared to fight in the streets for their cause. Military attacks were even encouraged by the pope for political purposes. The Guelphs were supportive of the pope, the spiritual power, while the Ghibellines supported the Holy Roman Emperor, the temporal power. Guelph and Ghibelline divisions were exacerbated by European powers as German Imperial States supported the claims of the emperor while France supported the Catholic pope.

In 1249, the Ghibellines conquered Florence and banished the Guelphs. However, when the Emperor Frederick II (a Ghibelline sympathiser) died in 1250, the Guelphs returned to Florence and regained control for the next ten years. The Ghibellines fought a famous battle at Montaperti in 1260 and Florence swung back to them. The Ghibellines killed 10,000 Guelphs and exiled numerous others from Florence and they razed Guelph towers, palaces and homes. Finally, in 1266, a year after Dante's birth, the Guelphs won a decisive victory and returned to Florence. The constant strife and dissent surrounding Dante's home city deeply affected him and through his writing he exacts revenge on the individuals he holds responsible. Purely statistically, he places 68 of his contemporaries in Hell compared with 19 in Purgatory and a mere 8 in Paradise.

Around the time the *Divine Comedy* is set in 1300, the Guelphs in Florence split into White Guelph and Black Guelph factions caused by a family quarrel in nearby Pistoia involving a brutal murder. Florentine Guelphs intervened by summoning the ringleaders to Florence and imprisoning them there. This only served to spread the feud to Florence. Rival family alliances were formed under the Black Donati (old blood) and the White Cerchi (rich and self-made), and these soon became politically divided. The White Guelphs wanted to have a government which was independent of the pope whereas the Black Guelphs supported the pope in his desire to influence government in Florence. Dante initially sided with the White Guelphs as he was very conscious of the abuse of power that the Catholic Church under the pope could wield if allowed to make laws to govern the people. He felt the Church should stick to its spiritual mission rather than interfere in material matters and law enforcement. For this reason, Dante puts a number of Black Guelphs and popes in Hell where they suffer endless torture.

Although Dante proclaimed himself a Guelph, his disappointment with persistent corruption in the Church weakened that alignment. He certainly had some sympathies with the Ghibelline cause, specifically in their patronage of the arts, their great leadership and their desire to see a united Italy akin to the ancient Empire, free from papal interference.

The other aspect of Dante's disappointment with life in Florence was the changing culture as a result of immigrating families seeking enrichment. Florence had become an economic and cultural powerhouse in Italy, but this newly created wealth attracted people whom Dante felt were outsiders. They included families who had never lived in Florence before and weren't loyal to it, who were just after a quick buck. Dante blames the Florentine nobles for allowing the city to be degraded in this way. Unsurprisingly, they also get rough treatment in Hell.

In 1300 Dante was appointed a prior which was a position similar to a city mayor and he exiled hundreds of violent rabble rousers from both White and Black Guelph factions in Florence. In a bid to ease the friction between the warring political parties, he was sent as an ambassador from Florence to Rome to plead with Pope Boniface VIII. However, Boniface, who supported the Black Guelphs, felt threatened and believed he could impose power more effectively through military force. He ordered Charles de Valois to send his troops to Florence to root out political subversives. Dante was accused of fraud, corruption and conspiracy against the pope and the Guelph party. Since Dante was in Rome at the time, he was exiled and prevented from returning to Florence for the rest of his life on pain of death.

He spent his time wandering Italy, staying with various friends, and he finished the *Divine Comedy* and his life at the house of his noble friend, Guido Novello da Polenta, in Ravenna where he died in 1321.

Hell Unearthed: language

My first motivation for writing *Hell Unearthed* was to adapt Dante's language for a modern audience. Dante chose to write the *Divine Comedy* in the vernacular or spoken Italian. This was revolutionary at the time as most high works of literature were written in Latin. His justification was to reach a wider public, not just the educated classes. Today, the *Divine Comedy* is rarely accessed by people other than students or teachers of Italian and so it is preserved in an exclusive domain which wasn't at all Dante's intention.

The language of Shakespeare and Dante will never change, and students will always have access to the original. However, I wanted to bring knowledge of Dante's work to a broader audience just as he intended at the time of writing. Dante wrote the *Divine Comedy* in terza rima, a three-line rhyming system. There have been scores of translations in both poetry and prose over the years, some quite literal and others more lyrical and playful. My first step was to complete my own translation-adaptation, remaining faithful to the text and its nuances. I wanted to achieve a balance between accessibility to the modern reader and a sense of the medieval heritage. Street language and the lexicon of banter dates very easily and I wanted to avoid a language so modern as to be short-lived. The second step was to move further away from the text and modernise the content while reinforcing Dante's themes and messages. This is something that has not been done before.

Sins

Dante was influenced by the philosopher Aristotle and the Christian theologian, Thomas Aquinas, in devising the schema for the *Divine Comedy*. The key concept is that sins of self-indulgence, where our passions lead us astray like lust, greed and anger, are not as bad as sins where we have used the gift of our intelligence to harm others, as in violence, fraud and treachery. Aristotle saw violence as a sort of mad bestiality with limited reason or intelligence applied. It therefore sits above fraud and treachery. Treachery which breaches bonds of love is the very worst sin of all. It inflicts the sharpest pain and demands the worst punishment.

Most people would broadly agree with this order of evil and the criminal justice system supports it as acts of lust or greed in themselves do not receive penalty whereas murder and theft do. Our social system has, however, evolved and some actions, once deemed sinful, are judged differently today. In Christian medieval times, sins included suicide, sorcery and sodomy. Witches were burned at the stake and anal sex was punished with castration, dismemberment or burning to death. Dante punished hypocrites and blasphemers in his Hell so there is scope for modernising the nature of some of these sins for our times.

In *Hell Unearthed*, you will find sinners engaged in honour-based violence and FGM; there are kidnappers, rapists, paedophiles, money launderers and human traffickers. They are punished more or less according to the rankings of modern criminal law, but they still sit within the original Aristotelian framework. Just like Dante, I have moulded the punishments the sinners suffer to the sin they perpetrated. The murderers are boiling away in a hot river of blood as they were in the original, but the paedophiles are buried in human excrement because they committed vile acts of indecency. The counterfeiters are forced to sit in chains while bank notes rain down around them as they made money out of forgeries.

Dante's key influences were drawn from central Europe, Islamic culture in Italy and the fights of the Crusades. I have expanded Dante's world in *Hell Unearthed* to show that people right across geographical, cultural and religious divides can be guilty of the same human failings. Recognition of the universality of sin should be a unifying process and I am sure that was also Dante's intention with the *Divine Comedy*.

Sinners

Dante fused fiction and non-fiction by drawing on characters from Greek and Roman history and mythology, from the Bible and from contemporary history. All of his characters would have been recognised by contemporary readers as they included public figures of the time as well as writers, poets, teachers, scientists and philosophers from ancient to medieval times. In order to engage the modern audience, I needed to draw on characters from recent times, either fictional or real and deceased.

In tune with our global world, I wanted to show how Dante's themes could apply not just in European quarters or in the Italy of his day, but across the world. Fortunately, Hell is a place for eternity and so it is timeless. It can incorporate characters from the past, present and future and this very nature adds to the universality of the work. Sin is part of human nature. It repeats itself through characters, through history and across nations.

Actually, sin cuts across religions too. Dante does have a pretty broad community in Hell and not all his chosen sinners are Catholic or even Christian. He includes characters from classical literature and other characters from the non-Christian world. Europe in his time had plenty of contact with Arabs and Muslims through years of conflict during the Crusades between Christians and Muslims. At the same time, the circulation of trade, goods and people with their ideas and knowledge resulted in cross-fertilisation of philosophy and literature. The Arab world translated Greek texts into Latin, and Arabic texts on science, astronomy, maths and medicine were brought to Italy via Spain and Sicily.

Dante places worthy Muslims, Ancient Greeks and non-Christians in Limbo because he recognises that not everyone feels able to follow his own Christian creed. They may not have hope of salvation, but neither are they punished within Hell. We see that the message he is trying to communicate has more to do with the nature of the sin and its consequences than the nature of the sinner. In the case of the characters in Limbo, the message is a celebration of human greatness irrespective of religion. With the same disregard for religion, I have reallocated Ulysses, the fictional character created by Homer, within the circle of fraud for having lied about the wooden horse. I have included Muslim sinners who held harmful beliefs and forced marriages or carried out FGM on family members. Adolf Hitler was born a Catholic, but he left Christianity behind as evil consumed him.

I have included more women in Hell than Dante. Dante did not think women were unworthy of inclusion. Quite the opposite. Not only is his ultimate inspiration and guide through the latter part of Purgatory and then Paradise embodied in Beatrice, the girl he met when he was only nine, but the lack of girls and women in Inferno at least, could be read as testament of a purer sex, free of sin relative to their male peers. In the interests of realism, and perhaps feminism, I have included female murderers, counterfeiters, and traitors. It is notable that, in my adaptation, there are many more female sinners guilty of the sins of self-indulgence than the sins of violence and fraud but, as sex has always oiled the cogs of the spy-world, there are quite a few engaged in treachery in the depths of Hell.

The structure of Hell Unearthed

The structure of *Hell Unearthed*, like Dante's *Inferno*, is a series of circles which lead to the earth's core where the Devil, Lucifer resides. The core itself is ice cold as it is the furthest reach from warm-blooded life. With each downwards spiral, the sins become more serious. At the perimeter of Hell, the Pagans and those who lived before Christ are placed in Limbo. Upper Hell contains the souls who have committed sins which are indulgences or human weaknesses (lust, greed and anger). Between Upper Hell and the main part of Hell are those who believed in harmful religious or cultural practices. The main part of Hell is contained within a region which I have renamed the City of Discord, harbouring the souls who have committed crimes of violence, fraud and treachery through malicious intent and of their own free will.

Cross-section of Hell

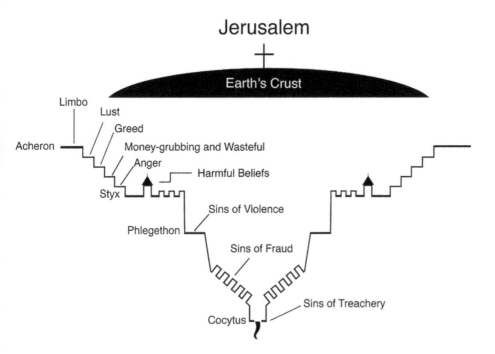

Relevance to the modern world

The principal targets of Dante's criticism in the Divine Comedy are of his own people and his country's system of faith and governance. It is the decadence he sees in the people of Florence, its politics and in the Catholic Church that aggrieve him above all. In Hell Unearthed, you will see criticism of governance as well as misguided cultures and extremism. Fundamentally, the sex, money and greed which poisoned Dante's world, continue to poison the world around us. And innocent people suffer.

Dante wants to impose order on the chaos of the world by categorising sin and the steps to redemption. Defining things is a natural human process as we try to understand the world around us. However, simplifying or putting things in boxes doesn't actually show us the truth in all its lights. Dante continually shows us that things are never black and white. Many of his cast of sinners are earthly heroes who have achieved greatness. They will have inspired their party followers, their countrymen, their students or their children. The *Divine Comedy* had Farinata, the Ghibelline leader who won an important victory at the battle of Montaperti in 1260. *Hell Unearthed* praises Horatio Nelson for leading the British navy to victory over Napoleon. But both men are thrown into the depths of Hell to suffer for where they went wrong. The overriding message is that earthly greatness is only temporary. It is the consequences of our moral conduct on earth which we carry with us for eternity.

People will make multiple and varied mistakes not just once, but time and time again. Which circle should they be allocated to when guilty of both infidelity and blackmail? The most offensive one or perhaps both? I have afforded both possibilities in my adaptation and have used artistic licence to distance myself from fixed judgements. After all, divine judgement is the only one that counts.

There is no doubt that both the detail and the big picture inspire plenty of topics for debate and, for me, this is the essence of the work and brings it alive. Dante filled the *Divine Comedy* with passion and love. He cared so much about his people and his country that he wanted us to see all the sores that had spoiled them and, beyond that, wider mankind and the world we live in. I hope that *Hell Unearthed* affords you a taste of that love and that, by exposing all that is wicked in society old and new, we may find a unifying motivation to make society and the world a safer, happier place to live. I hope that readers will find their own sources for debate because that is how we show that we are alive and that we care.

Map of Hell Unearthed

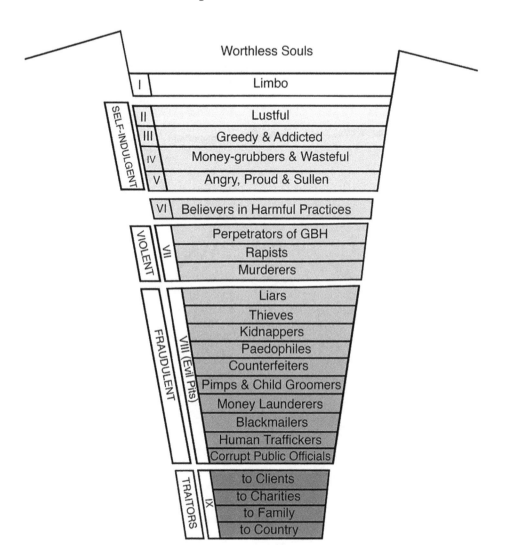

The Dark Wood

For some, it takes the death of a parent. For others, it is the sudden realisation that our children have physical or intellectual superiority. In any event, it happens to us all. We start to ponder the meaning of the life we have led and sense the burden of time passing and a responsibility to live our remaining years well. What will it be like to die, and will we be judged for our actions in life after we have died? Is it too late to lead a better life by giving back more to society and offering kindness and hope to our fellow citizens?

I had been ruminating on these things for many months and I felt alone and abandoned in the darkness of my mind. I was lost in a wild wood in the thick of night and entirely at the mercy of strange beasts whose hoots and howls shocked my senses. To save myself, I knew I had to find a ray of light. So, from this dark terror, I will try to lead you, dear reader, to a better, actually the best, place.

The mountain lit up with sun

I don't think I changed direction at any point. I just kept going, although I remember feeling utterly numbed by a deep fog of sleep. As I reached the edge of the fearful wood, a tall mountain, its summit initially shrouded in mist, came into view. I lifted my gaze and saw sunshine breaking through the smog until the whole mountain was tinged with golden rays. I felt the warmth penetrate my heart, immediately gladdening my spirits.

I was sure I had come to the right place and felt pulled towards the light. Fear and loneliness had previously held me down like heavy rocks in my heart. Now they suddenly dissipated like the mist. Determined as I was to leave my fear behind me, I couldn't resist turning back to face the wood to survey the extent of the evil I had left behind. I was like a sailor who has been spat out of his boat in a powerful storm and finally finds himself on the safety of the shore, but who cannot resist staring back into the salivating jaws of the waves.

I let my tired body ease into wakefulness and gathered myself to make the first hesitant steps up that deserted slope towards the light.

The three beasts

I blinked in the sunlight and almost tripped over myself when a flighty leopard leapt across my path. The colourful but vicious beast snarled in my face and looked poised to tear off a limb. By some blessing, she prowled in a wide circle in front of me, showing off her spectacular coat and didn't threaten me further. However, there didn't seem any way I could break past her clearly staked-out territory, and I wouldn't stand a chance if she decided to attack. For now, she seemed to enjoy showing off her splendour and strutting about, soaking up my horrified attention. As I marvelled in terror at her untouchable beauty, I thought of occasions when I had fallen to temptations of lust, greed or anger; the times when I had put my own desires before those of the people around me. How pathetic and weak that felt now!

The power of Nature strengthened me. Dawn was breaking and the spring sun rose majestically and unfalteringly in the sky. I drank in the rays of peace and happiness and for the first time I felt positive at the future. Even the beast before me with her radiant coat promoted this sense of positive purpose. The course seemed set, until a new feeling of dread began to bubble up inside me. I felt it before I saw it. A male lion, muscles rippling across his broad back, was approaching stealthily from the side. I saw from the corner of my eye that he held his head aloft and looked down his flaring nostrils as he examined me. He was troubled by my presence and started to emit a low growl. I immediately imagined scenes of ripped limbs, dishevelled bodies and spilled blood like a violent and merciless battle ground; and, as I trembled, the mountain trembled with me.

That wasn't the end of it. A third beast crossed my path. Now, a she-wolf, whose flanks barely disguised the spikes of her bony back, sloped towards me. She appeared delirious with hunger as saliva dripped from her sharp fangs, and she rolled her eyes in a fit of spasm. I was afraid I may be her first dish in a long while. I feared for my life, as here was an animal that would stop at nothing to get her way. No loyalty, no respect, no charity. Only treachery and fraud as a means to an end. At this point, I was so filled with dread that I lost all hope of making it up the mountain to the warm embrace of the sun's rays. I was so close and could see the prize before my eyes, but a dark curtain had fallen yet again, and this uncompromising beast drove me back from the place of light to the place of despicable darkness.

Virgil appears

I retreated as fast as my weary legs could carry me. Soon, I caught sight of the eerie branches at the edge of the wood beckoning me with their gnarled fingers, and I perceived a faint figure lurking in the shadows. To be sure that my imagination wasn't getting the better of me, I shouted out, 'Get away from me, ghost, or, if you are a living thing, then lend me a helping hand!'

I stopped in my tracks as the figure stepped towards me, yet still it was not clear whether he was ghoul or man. But then he spoke in a clear and confident voice and revealed, 'It is true that I am no longer alive. I was born and raised in Mantua in Lombardy soon after the death of Julius Caesar but a good seventy years before Christ's time. I was the poet who sang of glorious Troy and its terrible destruction by the wanton Greeks; of Aeneas, the son of noble Anchises, who was forced to flee the burning rubble. Now listen, stop what you are doing! Why are you running back to the place where all your troubles began? You need to head straight back up that mountain towards the light, which is the only true path to happiness.'

I knew at once that I was talking to my hero, Virgil, the poet of classical literature who had inspired so many writers with his work, the *Aeneid*. I have always admired his stories of ancient Greeks and Romans infused with classical myths which he relates so enchantingly. I was desperate to show off my knowledge of his work in an act of deference.

'My Lord, I cannot imagine how this auspicious meeting has come about. You have taught me so much and my fame wouldn't be possible without you. But please, wise Virgil,' I implored through plaintive tears, 'have you not seen that terrible beast which has driven me back to the darkness? Can you save me from her ferocious fangs because I have no weapons against her?'

Virgil didn't seem phased by my fear and angst and he rallied me with clear instructions. 'If you are determined to leave your sorrows and this wretched darkness behind you, then you have to change direction. There is no way past that vicious creature. She intends to devour you, and the more lives she destroys, the more she craves. You need a new path now.'

Virgil's prediction about the greyhound

Virgil explained how the she-wolf had cast her spell over many people through the ages, causing them to commit acts of treachery and fraud: sins which break the fundamental bonds of trust in society and create irreparable divisions.

But he also spoke of a saviour greyhound who would be able to hunt down any evil perpetrators and, with supreme authority, would restore order and respect in society, laying down laws to bind nations together. 'The greyhound will not feed on material things but on faith, hope and charity and he will be born of humble cloth. He will redeem Italy, the country where both the emperor and the pope take their seats, and he will drive the she-wolf from every corner of the land. The beast will be banished with her tail between her legs, and she will be sent back to Hell from where envy first unleashed her.'

The journey to the underworld

My eyes brightened as hope radiated through my body. Virgil offered me a warm embrace and spoke to me like a father. 'To set you off on the right course, I'd like you to follow me. I will show you, first, the place of misery that all men fear after death. It is true that the abyss of Hell is filled with wailings and all sorts of unimaginable torments, but to really see into yourself you must witness that terror at first hand and then you can be a better person. Next, you will see souls in Purgatory who accept the burning flames which surround them with a joyful attitude as they know they are close to their journey's final leg when they will be reunited with God, their maker. I do not have the ability to lead you onwards to Paradise as I was never part of the Christian world, but if you want to journey that far then I will entrust you into the hands of a more suitable guide. She is your childhood love, Beatrice, whose grace and beauty allow her a seat in the realm of Paradise. There you will see the health, happiness and bounty that occupy God's kingdom.'

Encouraged by his warmth and assertiveness, I asked him to lead me on. 'Virgil, I will be forever grateful to you for showing me the way out of the clutches of these terrifying monsters who are trying to ensnare me. Lead me to the underworld with the suffering souls so that I may find St Peter's gates and the cleansing place of Purgatory.'

He wrapped his cloak around his shoulders and beckoned me on. I followed dutifully in his wake, eager to match his stride.

Dante's Mental Struggle

A vision of the afterlife was granted only to Aeneas, Virgil's fictional character in the Aeneid, and to Saint Paul in the Bible. Aeneas was elected by God to found Rome, capital of the Empire and seat of the Catholic Church. Saint Paul was elected to establish the Christian Church on earth in order to lead people to salvation. Why would such a privilege be granted to an ordinary man like Dante? Dante justifies this special treatment by explaining that Beatrice (his personal inspiration and literary muse), elevated alongside the Virgin Mary, was the one who implored Virgil to rescue her desperate friend. We can all share the experience of this divinely willed journey because we are ordinary just like Dante. We, too, will undergo the process of recognising our sins, cleansing ourselves and finally reaching redemption. We are about to embark on the first stage of this journey.

Dante's fears

Daylight was beginning to fade. Ordinary people would be downing tools for the evening and readying themselves for rest and relaxation. In contrast, my exertions were just beginning. I was embarking on a journey that would take me through a mass of misery and terror, provoking pity, horror and grief. As I retell the story now, I have an instinctive desire to push the memory away, but the vision was so vivid that I am going to set it all down for you faithfully here.

My first concern was to try to understand why I of all people should be chosen to undertake this journey to the underworld with the protection of my all-time hero. Perhaps there had been some mistake.

'Dear Virgil, before we take our first steps on this important adventure, can you explain how it is I have been granted this privilege? I can see why Aeneas should be granted access to the land of the dead as his achievements were truly great. After all, he founded Rome, and from there the Roman Empire and ultimately, Christianity. You told us the story of how Aeneas heard the prophecy that drove him to victory in Rome. That victory led to the establishment of papal authority in Rome and later, God's messenger, Saint Paul, arrived there to confirm the Christian faith and show us the path to salvation. What have I got on that? I am nothing to either Aeneas or Saint Paul and can hardly see a reason why I should be chosen for this journey. How did it all come about and how did you find me? I am sure you have the answers to help me understand.'

The more I thought about the situation, the more unnerved I felt. I swung from hopeless fear to adrenalin-fuelled excitement and back again and my mind spun in circles of indecision and uncertainty.

Comfort from Virgil and support from Beatrice

For the second time, Virgil came to my aid. 'Listen, Dante, I can imagine what you are thinking and feeling but don't let your fears get the better of you, and don't let your imagination cloud your judgement here. I can explain everything, and then you can rest assured. Now that I am long dead, I reside in a part of Hell called Limbo where souls are suspended in the air. We are not punished as sinners simply because we existed before Christian times and therefore had no knowledge of sin or salvation. Sadly, that also means we will never know the fruits of Paradise, but at least we are not subjected to terrible torments like other souls. Anyway, a few days ago, the most graceful and angelic lady you have ever seen came to ask me a favour and, going weak at the knees, I couldn't wait to oblige her. The radiant light in her eyes captivated me and her voice was blessed and simply beautiful. She asked that I rescue her dear, faithful and true friend from the worries of his ways and guide him back to the rightful path. She said you were frightened in the wilderness and caught out by insurmountable terrors which thwarted your attempt to find some light, driving you back to a dark place. She feared it was too late and that you were too far gone in the wilderness to be rescued or, worse, had been attacked by the beasts and left for dead. She said she was moved by love to help you and asked me to use my way with words to persuade you to undertake this journey of salvation. I was so overcome with inspiration to fulfil her request that I felt ready to push myself to the ends of the earth!'

Virgil explained how Beatrice had come to Limbo from Heaven, remaining untouched by the fires of Hell as her blessed nature protects her from wounds of the flesh. She had sought permission for this endeavour from the gentle Virgin Mary who takes pity on sinners who have lost their way when there is hope of regaining the true path. Virgil told me that when the angels urged Beatrice to come to my assistance, she sped with all her might to find him in Limbo, hopeful that his words could induce me to find the right way.

Virgil continued, 'Beatrice's eyes glistened with tears as she implored me to help you. Her passion propelled me more quickly to your side. Now, listen, I have come to your rescue and I have saved you from the beasts which filled you with fear. You know you can trust me. Summon up some courage and try to toughen up! You have blessed ladies in the highest heavens fighting for your cause and I have promised to guide and protect you. You put your trust in my written words, why not embrace my spoken reassurances?'

Dante's renewed strength of purpose

Imagine little flowers whose petals curl in on themselves to fend off the night chill and then slowly unfurl and stand up tall as the morning sun warms them. I felt like those petals as renewed determination restored strength to my body, and I said, 'I am touched and grateful to be under the watchful eye of such gracious and special people, and I feel as ready to follow you now as I did at the outset, before silly anxieties set my mind wandering. Come on, let's get going. I am happy to appoint you leader, lord and master.'

Those are precisely the words I said to him, and so our journey on the rough, wild path into the abyss began.

The Gate of Hell; Unworthy Souls; the River Acheron

Dante and Virgil arrive at the gate of Hell and just inside they come across souls who have achieved nothing in their lives. They have not sinned but neither have they contributed to society. They have sat on the fence all their lives either because they don't have a care or because they are undecided on their course of action. Surely, we should live life to the full through actions designed to help the community and for the public good?

They then come to the river Acheron where all the damned souls gather after death awaiting the ferryman, Charon, to take them across.

The gate of Hell

THROUGH ME YOU ENTER THE SORROWFUL CITY,

THROUGH ME YOU ENTER INTO ETERNAL SUFFERING,

THROUGH ME YOU WILL JOIN THE LOST SOULS.

JUSTICE MOVED MY BLESSED MAKER.

CREATED BY GOD ABOVE I AM THE FATHER,

THE SON AND THE HOLY GHOST,

ENDOWED WITH POWER, WISDOM AND JUSTICE.

BEFORE ME NOTHING WAS CREATED EXCEPT

ETERNAL THINGS, AND ETERNAL AM I.

ABANDON ALL HOPE, YOU WHO ENTER HERE.

These leaden letters were etched above a tall gate made of iron, flaking with rust that heralded the decay of what lay within. I couldn't grasp their meaning, but Virgil, my kind and gentle master, said, 'Be brave, Dante. We are about to witness a world of pain and suffering. You will see souls who are being punished for their wrongdoings in life with torments that must last for eternity.'

Virgil took my hand in his, and the warmth of his kindness comforted me as we set off together to uncover the path ahead.

Souls moved to neither good deeds nor bad

As soon as we had passed through the grim gate, my ears were filled with sighing and loud wailing sounds. Looking up at the starless sky, I felt all bravery abandon me. What was this alien and unfamiliar world? I was aware of shrill and angry voices on the one hand and feeble, pained moans on the other. I heard contorted voices speaking languages I could not recognise. The sound of slapping hands unsettled me, and I felt dizzy in the swirling cacophony which filled that black and timeless air.

'Who are these souls who seem so overwhelmed with suffering and sadness?' I asked. 'What terrible thing have they done that brings them to weep such bitter tears?'

Virgil was quick to answer me. 'Have no pity for these contemptible souls. They did nothing of value in their lives. They chose not to go out of their way to help their neighbours or make society a better place. Everyone can make a difference, however small, and this lot did nothing for the people around them. They could only think about themselves, so they are forced to suffer meaninglessly and alone. By the same token, they didn't harm anybody, so they are only placed in the outskirts of Hell. Heaven doesn't want them in case they taint its beauty and Hell doesn't want them either in case they dilute its evil. In life, they deserved no recognition, no pity, no respect. Let's not waste any further time on them. You can look at them but let's move on quickly by.'

Of course, I did look at the band of souls and was surprised to see a flag bearer running in circles with a green banner billowing about above his head. A long column of souls trailed behind him like a giant centipede dancing on hot coals. I was shocked by the number of indolent sinners who had been captured here. Among them, I recognised Pope Celestine V who gave up the papacy after only five months because he didn't feel up to the job. The worst part of this abdication of responsibility was that it opened the way for the most evil pope ever, Pope Boniface VIII, to take over the papal seat. This man abused his power in the church, filling it with corruption. Rather than focus on the spiritual mission of the church, he interfered with politics in Florence and, on account of him, I feared for my future.

Anger welled up within me as I thought about these woeful popes, but I felt merely indifferent to the souls surrounding me who did nothing to either please or offend. As we passed closely by, I could see that they were hopping about stark naked, veiled by a cloud of horseflies and wasps which were vying to threaten them. These sorry souls had lacked any stimulus to take action in life, but now they were stung into eternal sensation. Streams of blood ran down their faces which, mixed with their free-flowing tears, provided an abundant feast for the hungry worms gathering in wait at their feet.

The river Acheron and Charon

I looked ahead in the feeble light and saw a crowd of figures on the bank of a great river, converging in eager anticipation at the water's edge like young revellers at a concert. I asked Virgil to tell me who they were. 'You have so many questions! Just be patient and it will all become clear when we get closer. That is the river Acheron.'

I felt ashamed of my eagerness and I certainly didn't want to bother my worthy leader unduly. I kept my eyes fixed on my shoes to keep curiosity at bay and held my tongue until we reached the river.

A sharp swooshing noise swept through the water in front of us and, looking up, I saw a boat speeding towards the shore. Standing at the helm was an old white-haired man with a broad and bristling beard and fiery, red eyes. He raised his oar in the direction of the heaving souls and shouted, 'Hey there, you pitiful wretches! Don't be so eager to cross this river as no joy awaits you on the other side, and you won't be getting out of here to see the sun or the stars! I have been instructed to take you across the river where you will be greeted by eternal shadows, fire and ice.

'And who is that?' he called, pointing the oar at me. 'This is no place for a living creature. Be off with you! You have no business here and you certainly can't come on board my boat!'

Virgil intervened at this point and said, 'Charon, you don't understand. Put down your oar and listen to me. This man has been brought here by divine will and you have no power against that, so on board your boat he will go!'

The ferryman of the murky marsh let his oar drop to his side and fell silent, but the wheels of fire continued to turn in his eyeballs and puffs of smoke poured out of his ears, conveying his still-fuming anger.

As my eyes switched from the demon, Charon, to the souls on the bank, I noticed that they were starting to change colour, and their teeth chattered as they absorbed the cruel ferryman's words. They cursed their bad fortune and now they wished they had never been born. Heaving with laboured sobs, they huddled together on that miserable bank awaiting their destiny of fire or ice.

Charon's eyes were now glowing like coals and he beckoned the gathering souls to approach his boat. Without hesitation, he used his oar to strike any sorry souls who lingered anxiously behind, and they leapt on board the boat. By the time the vessel had carried its burden to the far shore, a new crowd was pressing up to the water's edge, keen to leave the plaintive cries of the unworthy souls behind them.

Virgil started to tell me about the souls we had met on the bank. 'My dear son, you won't recognise or understand every one of these souls as they come from all corners of the world. They are gathered here because their choices in life have disappointed their divine maker. They know that divine justice demands punishment for their wrongdoings and, eager to get it over and done with, their fear turns to desire to cross the river Acheron and submit to their torment. Every soul passing here has committed an evil act so, if Charon treats you cruelly, now you know why.'

The earthquake and Dante's faint

Still shocked by the plight of these sinners, I became aware of a trembling deep in the earth's core. Suddenly the dark mass beneath us shook so violently that fear bathes me in sweat even now. A gale whipped up from the tear-drenched ground and lightning flashed a beam of crimson in the darkness. My heart pounded in my chest until I felt nothing more, and I dropped unconscious to the ground.

CANTO 4

Limbo

Limbo, the first circle of Hell, is for unbaptised souls and those Pagans who, because they came before Christ's time, did not know God. It also includes baptised souls who are no longer certain in their faith. They have not committed a sin of the flesh or of the mind and therefore they balance on the fringes of Hell. Limbo contains many morally virtuous and inspirational individuals who do not follow Christian dogma. They are afforded a beautiful resting place after death but, without Christianity in their lives, they are deprived any hope of salvation.

Limbo

A loud thunderclap broke my slumber, and I was jolted awake as though someone was shaking me by the shoulders, urging me into action. For a moment, I had forgotten where I was, so I took a moment to come to my senses. Surrounded by a dark, deep fog, my receptors were limited, and I could barely see beyond my nose. I was aware, however, that I was standing on the edge of a huge black abyss filled with the din of eternal wailing. Immediately my eyes strained for my trusted companion and guide.

Virgil came to my side to reassure me although his face was drained of colour. 'It's time to descend into the blind world below. The path is narrow and rugged so I will go first. You can follow in my footsteps.'

'How am I supposed to make this journey with you when you are clearly terrified even before we have started on our way?' I lamented.

'It is not fear that I am feeling but, rather, pity at the multitude of souls who are tormented here. Muster up some courage and trust me. I will take good care of you. Now let's get going. We have a long journey ahead of us.'

With these words, we set off for the first circle, called Limbo, which surrounds the abyss.

As we approached the souls gathered in the first circle, I was struck by a different sound being carried through the air. There was no longer wailing or crying but, rather, a constant sighing which swirled through the fog like a gentle breeze, making the air tremble around us. These spirits of men, women and children were not suffering any physical torment, but they were grieving out of eternal sadness. Virgil explained that these lost souls, like himself, had done nothing wrong in life but, through no fault of their own, many had never been baptised. They either existed before Christ's time or they didn't follow the Christian faith, so they suffer eternal sadness because they know there is no hope of salvation.

My heart went out to these souls as I knew many of them had achieved remarkable things in life through their work in science, literature and world peace and yet here they were, suspended in Limbo.

When I asked Virgil if anyone from this place had made it to Heaven, he was ready with an answer: 'Not long after I arrived here, I saw the Almighty Father, crowned with the victory of the resurrection and shrouded in a powerful light. He collected a number of souls we know from the Old Testament such as Adam, father of the human race, Abraham, the father of Judaism, Christianity and Islam, and Moses, who revealed the Ten Commandments to the people. Other than them, no one has been brought to salvation from Limbo.'

The great Greek and Roman poets of classical literature

The souls were standing tall, their heads held high, and their minds focused on their discussion. They were grouped closely in circles like trees in a series of copses scattered about the plain. As I peered through the shadows at the figures gathered there, my eyes were drawn to a small fire giving off a faint glow in the middle of the plain. The light from the fire shone onto the faces of the closest circle of souls and, as I leant in to recognise their features, I heard one of them speak. 'We welcome honourable Virgil whose spirit was departed from us but has now returned!'

The air grew still and silent and four souls dressed in brightly coloured robes stepped forward into the light of the fire. Virgil pointed out Homer who wrote the famous poems called the *Iliad* and the *Odyssey*, foundational works of classical literature. Homer held a sword in his hand to remind us of the bloodshed endured in the siege of Troy and, as he nodded to his fellow souls, I heard him say, 'Words as empty as the wind are best left unsaid.'

Alongside Homer, Virgil picked out Horace, the famous Roman poet, whose words reached my ears. 'We are but dust and shadow.' The final two great Roman poets were Ovid, creator of the mythological *Metamorphoses,* and Lucan. Ovid beckoned to Virgil to join them in conversation saying, 'Time is the devourer of all things.' They looked set to fall into a deep discussion on life and the human condition when Homer turned to me and invited me into their group to stay a while. Virgil gave me a broad grin of satisfied approval and I felt overwhelmed with pride and honour at being recognised by them and judged worthy to join in their deliberations.

The castle of the great and good

Having left the wise poets and their musings behind us, we soon arrived at the foot of a magnificent castle whose turrets rose out of the shadows. I counted seven high walls made of golden stone encircling the castle with a moat, filled with clear water, further defending the outermost perimeter. Virgil and I followed the well-tended path through all seven gates, admiring the splendour of the construction. Gargoyles and engravings decorated the gates depicting human toil, labour and achievement. In one image, a man studied the stars with his telescope and, alongside him, a rocket was heading straight for the moon.

Inside the castle we came to an enchanting green meadow smelling of freshly cut grass and bordered by the most beautiful blue and white wildflowers. Souls walked steadily and with profound composure, as though deep in thought, as they crossed the lawn. They held books, instruments or drawings in their hands as sources of discussion, and I sensed immediately the very real and bountiful talent displayed before me.

Virgil led me up some steps onto an elevated stone platform running along one side of the meadow, giving us a perfect vantage point for the whole scene set out below. From here, there was enough light to make out a raft of great and good souls and, to be faced with such talent and success from the past and from the future, made me tingle with excitement.

From the ancient world, I saw the great physicians, Hippocrates, Avicenna and Galen, as well as Averroës, the doctor and influential Arab philosopher.

Here I set my eyes on future pioneers of magnetism and radiation, Pierre and Marie Curie and Albert Einstein who was to develop the theory of relativism. There was Gorbachev, with his birthmarked scalp, who would be renowned for his work in promoting peace between Russia and its neighbours and putting an end to the Cold War.

Virgil pointed out the musical genius of the future, David Bowie, describing him as a fan of both my writing and Homer's in equal measure. I was flattered by the compliment and asked Virgil to tell me more about this new soul. Virgil explained that David Bowie was in Limbo because he refused to put his spirituality in a single box. He advocated changes, not through indecision, but because he was constantly exploring new things. He would embrace the future by supporting advances in technology and space exploration. Here in Limbo, he enjoyed discussions with his literary heroes like Homer. He told Virgil all about the sinners of the future so that my guide was well-versed in the characters who were filling the grim abyss below. David Bowie would be each of a Buddhist, a Christian, an agnostic and an atheist, and yet none of them. Even his eyes couldn't be pinned down as one was blue and the other, a much darker colour.

I was shown the Dalai Lamas who would stand for religious harmony and tolerance, Mahatma Gandhi who would famously advocate non-violent resistance to authority and inspire campaigns for civil rights and freedom across the world. I also noted Meena who would establish the Revolutionary Association of Women in Afghanistan in order to give a voice to deprived and silenced women. She fought for equality and education for women until she was brutally assassinated, but her organisation lives on.

To list them all here would take far too long, and you will be eager to hear about the rest of my journey but be sure that there were many more heroes of humanity than I have noted here.

Virgil and I descended from our observation point and left the buzzing hive of debate and deliberation to follow a different path leading out of the castle courtyard, back into the trembling air where no light shines.

Lustful

Buffeted about by the Wind

Dante and Virgil now descend to the second circle of Hell and the first for sins of self-indulgence or human weakness.

Minos

Back on the edge of the dark void we descended into the second circle of Hell which, I noticed, was smaller than the first. The spiral seemed to shrink just as the pain and suffering contained within its rings seemed to increase. Before I could lay eyes on the suffering souls within, I was stopped in my tracks by an enormous human monster. He rippled and flexed his muscles across his limbs, snarling at the queue of sinners who stood in line timidly at his feet, his fangs glistening. Trailing behind him was a long and powerful reptilian tail which oozed venomous gloop at his feet. Minos was his name, and with his grim crown on his head, he sat in judgement over these hellish sinners.

One by one, the sinners were made to confess their misdeeds to Minos, and, with a twinkle of his eye, he would consider the truth of their statements. Next, he would coil his tail around his middle, once, twice or three times, corresponding to the number of the circle to which he was dispatching the sinner. With a flash of his unfurling tail, the sinners received their judgement and were hurled down into the abyss below.

When Minos saw me, he paused in his duties a moment and said, 'Watch your back, stranger to these parts, you can't trust anyone around here. Don't be tempted to get too close, the gates to Hell are wide open!'

Virgil put himself between us and asserted his authority saying, 'Minos, enough of your provocation! You don't have the power to change what has been authorised from above, so leave him be!'

The lustful

Once we had navigated our way around Minos, the sound of sorrowful crying rose up again and made my ears redden with pain and pity. The wails were captured by a powerful wind which roared like a raging storm and, as I approached the scene, I could see souls buffeted about by the hellish hurricane. Their bodies were helplessly hurled about by the angry wind this way, that way, up, down and sideways. The gale swept them up high in the air and then smashed them down to the ground in endless torment.

Virgil explained that these souls had given way to indomitable passion. Frequently, lust spiralled out of control breaching social and moral norms because reason had failed to rein it in. I stepped forward, eager to hear the stories of these sorry souls, their physical plight already tugging at my heart strings.

A black cloud of whirling souls barrelled its way towards us, and I asked Virgil to tell me who they were. 'These souls have all succumbed to extreme passion which was fraught due to the customs and accepted norms where they lived, but their passion lasted till the end. The one wearing a royal diadem on her head is Cleopatra, Queen of Egypt, who fell in love with the Roman general Mark Antony and killed herself in order to avoid being taken prisoner by her enemy, Octavian. Next to her is Helen of Troy who fell for Paris despite being married to the King of Sparta, Menelaus. You will also see Romeo and Juliet whose loves straddled the feuding families of the Montagues and the Capulets and culminated in their tragic deaths. The one with the hunchback is Quasimodo, the legendary bell ringer of Notre Dame Cathedral. His unrequited love for Esmeralda came to a head when she was falsely hung for murder, although he was later buried in her tomb. The good-looking one in the smart jacket is Edward VIII, who was very briefly King of England before choosing to abdicate the throne and leave duty behind in order to marry the love of his life, Wallis Simpson. It was a scandal at the time because she was a divorcée who came from a country in the west that the world will come to know as America.'

Virgil pointed out thousands of souls who had died with tragic passion in their hearts and named them all. I felt truly sorry for each and every one as love is such a beautiful thing even though it can lead to heartbreak and sorrow. I listened carefully to all these stories of love and felt as though the wicked wind had whipped up my mind as a second spate of dizziness overcame me.

Lady Diana, Princess of Wales

I was drawn to two souls who seemed wrapped in their own ball of wind. Their bodies were intertwined, locked in an embrace with their hands tightly clasped. Virgil anticipated my interest and encouraged me to talk to them. 'In a few moments, they will be buffeted in our direction. Just call out to them and, guided by love, they will stop to talk with you.'

As they whirled towards us, I chose my moment to raise my voice. 'I can see you are blessed to be together as you are, but please tell me how you came to be here as I am keen to learn your story.'

The cloud they were encased in like a pair of turtle doves swirled about in front of us and slowed to a drift at our feet. 'We have heard your plea to talk to us and take great solace in the concern and interest you have shown for our cause. For as long as the wind draws breath, we will stay a while and talk with you. I am Diana. I endured fifteen years of marriage when my husband's eyes were always for another woman. I felt affectionate towards him and wanted to make the marriage that I had signed up to work. However, it became increasingly clear that I had fallen into a marriage of convenience whose main purpose was to provide an heir to the British throne.

My husband's barely concealed infidelity pushed me further and further away from him and I sought solace in the arms of men who could show me the affection I so badly needed. See how I am punished for my indiscretions now. We divorced eventually and, a year later, I fell into the arms of this man who was besotted with my beauty. Passion destroyed my marriage but now I had found someone who could love me untainted. However, the world wouldn't let it go. I guessed at his intentions in life, but he was indeed resolved to ask for my hand in marriage and had bought an engagement ring inscribed with the words "dis-moi oui". Love is quick to take root in a kind heart and the intensity of our love continues to afflict me, but it couldn't live long because fate took it all violently away. Love joined us together in a single sudden death and we will not be separated now.'

Diana's words touched me deeply and I thought about how both illicit and true passion could lead to such pain and tragedy. I raised my head and looked directly at the pair of lovers. 'Diana, your suffering makes me want to weep, particularly as you have suffered so much in life, in death, and even now after death. I am intrigued to know if you can tell me when you first felt love and how could you be sure it was true?'

Diana spoke again, 'I cannot express the pain of thinking back over those final months of happiness in life when it is impossible to escape such a place of shadows and darkness as this. Your guide and teacher will understand. Still, your persistence deserves an answer, and I am bound to satisfy your kind curiosity, so here goes. You will hear it through my pain and tears. We were holidaying on a boat in the hot summer sun and we moored up just outside a beautiful rocky cove. Next, we dived into the clear turquoise water and saw starfish on the sea bed and little fish flashing their blue and yellow bodies beneath us. Back on board the boat, we made ourselves a picnic on our towels and fell to talking about the beauty of unspoiled things, how short life is, and the importance of treasuring moments of happiness so that they might endure.

As we spoke, we felt the need for connection, for real value in our lives and suddenly felt that we may have found it. Arriving at this realisation together, we recognised love was at work. At that moment, this man, who shall never be parted from me, laid his lips on my mouth in a tender kiss. That was true happiness, true love.'

All the while Diana related her story, the other soul poured out tears in heartache and I was so troubled by their pain that I faded away, falling to the ground like a dead weight.

CANTO 6

Greedy and Addicted

Submerged in Mud under Driving Rain

Greed or excessive consumption whether of food, drugs or alcohol, is a sort of solitary self-indulgence and so these souls resemble beasts who grovel alone in the mud with no awareness of the souls around them. The Florentine soul, Ciacco, prophesies political mayhem in Florence. He conveys Dante's disappointment with civil unrest in Florence and the fall of the White Guelphs. Blame falls on the arrogance of noble families as well as the greed of the new mercantile classes. Dante also meets characters from the future who consumed to excess and met with premature deaths.

Cerberus

I regained consciousness with Virgil leaning over me, slapping me gently around the cheeks. I slowly regained my feet and my senses. The tenderness and pity I had felt for the kindred spirits behind me now hardened as I became aware of new torments, and I braced myself to face human fallibility of a different sort.

I had reached the third circle in the abyss of Hell and here a cursed, cold and constant rain drove down like stabbing blades. Black rain, snow and rocks of hail bucketed down through the murky air and the soaked earth gave off a foul stench.

Looming over the wretched souls soaked in sickly slime was Cerberus, the monstrous dog with three throats. His thunderous barks were enough to explode the ears of any soul who dared to raise his head above the filth in which they were submerged. His eyes were crimson pools of blood and his beard was steeped in a greasy, black slime. His pot belly was as taut as a drum and his hands were talons with which he clawed, hacked and ripped the flesh of those captured in his cage.

Like the beast who kept them in their state of terror, the souls resembled tormented dogs as the piercing rain cut into their bodies and made them howl in pain. I saw them wriggle and roll from one flank to the other to dilute their suffering.

Noticing Virgil and me for the first time, Cerberus fell silent for a moment as he lifted his shaggy head to check us over. He suddenly opened his jaws to reveal his blood-stained fangs and his whole body quivered in desperate craving. Virgil knelt down, scooped a fistful of stony slurry into his cupped hands and hurled the grit into those ravenous throats. Just as a baying starved dog is silenced at the first bite of food, so the squalid muzzles of craving Cerberus were mollified.

Souls driven to excess; Ciacco and his prophecy

We passed over souls who were beaten into the mud by the driving rain and it was hard not to tread on their bodies. Among those lying in the squalor, Virgil showed me the singer, Elvis Presley, who was to become an icon of the twentieth century: the "King of Rock and Roll". He was equally famous for eating towers of peanut butter and jam sandwiches, but it was his overindulgence in prescription drugs which led to his premature death. Next was William Makepeace Thackery, author of Vanity Fair, who was to die of his gluttony, and the footballer, George Best who, despite his speed and control of the ball, couldn't control his alcoholism. As a result, they all carried a new and eternal burden in the afterlife.

One of the souls scrambled to his feet as soon as he saw us approaching and spoke directly to me. 'I am sure I know who you are. Do you recognise me? I have not been in this murky place for long and our lives will have overlapped.'

I peered at his features for a clue to help me check his claim, but the casing of mud on his face presented only a mask. 'I have no idea who you could be. You are disguised by your wretched state, but why don't you tell me about yourself so that I understand more about your suffering and what brought you to this dreadful place? You may not be the worst of this evil bunch in Hell, but surely the stench can't get worse than this.'

The soul continued, 'I know your city well as I also spent my short life there. There is so much greed for wealth and power among our fellow citizens that hands are always grasping for more and people are never satisfied with their lot. The people of Florence nicknamed me Ciacco and here I am, lashed by rain for the disease of excessive eating. I suffer alone but there are many souls in the same sorry position who are paying for excessive consumption of whatever it may be that they craved beyond moderation.'

I felt a certain sympathy for my fellow Florentine; his words chimed true. 'Ciacco, I am sorry to see you and your fellow sufferers laid low like pigs in this slime. As souls like you can now see the future and the fate of future sinners, can you tell me more about the future of my beloved city of Florence? What will happen to the people living there while the feuding and civil unrest persists?'

'I can tell you that they will fight it out for years to come in terror and with bloodshed. People will flee their homes and lose their livelihoods. The White Guelphs will drive out the Blacks, hurling insults as they go. However, within three years, the Whites are destined to fall, and the Blacks will rise again, propelled to power by the person who claims that he doesn't favour either side. Yes, I think you can guess, that person is Pope Boniface. That evil pope will be the source of great sadness to you as he will banish you from Florence for obstructing his political dominance. From that point on, the Blacks will lord it over the Whites keeping them crushed under their thumbs despite their protests. As for the few remaining respectable people in government there, I am afraid nobody listens to them. Pride, envy and greed are the three evil seeds which have poisoned people's hearts.'

For some time now, I had feared that Pope Boniface would damage my future in Florence, but I was still struck by the weight of Ciacco's prophecy. I was eager to hear more and pushed him further. 'Please tell me about our great leaders, warriors and politicians, who commanded respect through their commitment to improve people's lives and make society a better place? Are they enjoying the sweetness of Heaven or the bitterness of Hell?'

'Despite the great inventions, strategic responses, public policies and social support systems delivered by a number of talented people in public life, many of them are down in the blackest depths of Hell. They are weighed down by wrongdoings which, let's face it, afflict most of the human race, and they are punished after death accordingly. You will find them all here in this dark abyss if you manage to make it all the way down to the bottom. I have told you what you wanted to know, and in exchange, I'd like you to remind people about me back on earth when you return to the green and pleasant land.'

Ciacco kept his gaze on me, longing for some attachment to life which was no longer his to share. He strained his eyes for so long that he became cross-eyed, dropped his head to his chest and flopped back into the filth among the other blinded souls.

What happens on Judgement Day

As we walked slowly on together through the filthy slurry, I asked Virgil about the destiny of these sinning souls. I was fascinated to learn more about the afterlife. How did the souls sense their pain and was their suffering truly eternal?

Virgil explained, 'These souls will only wake up when the angelic trumpet sounds on the Judgement Day at the end of time. On that day, the Holy One will arrive and each soul shall be reunited with the coffin they were buried or cremated in. Each soul will be reclothed in flesh and human form and, at the gong, they will hear their eternal sentence. They will be returned to one of Hell, Purgatory or Paradise. Once they are reunited with their bodies, they will feel more keenly the effects of either punishment or blessedness because they will be perfected forms again. Right now, these souls are detached from the flesh of their bodies which remains buried on earth. They are imperfect forms at the moment and, whilst their cries of pain are terrible, that pain will only intensify at the end of time when they assume perfect forms again.'

I was grateful for the knowledge that Virgil imparted to me, but it made my heart heavy and my steps became sluggish and slow. Seeing these souls submit to their torments, I yearned to find strength in my heart and mind to only do good in life so that I might be blessed rather than punished. At last, we found a path down to the fourth circle.

And here, we found Pluto, the devil's own god of wealth.

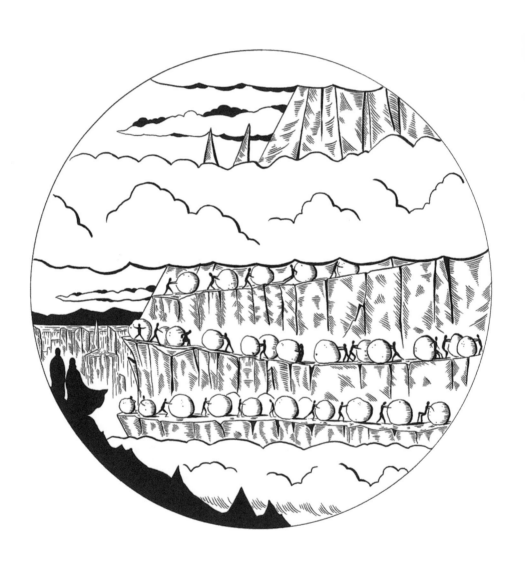

CANTO 7

Money-grubbers and Wasteful

Rolling Heavy Boulders

As Dante meets the souls of the money-grubbing and wasteful, he is drawn to think about the role of Fate, how wealth is distributed amongst mankind on earth and how power is held by one political party rather than another.

Pluto

'Well, well, Satan, prince of Devils, and who do we have here?' mocked Pluto from his vast throne of gold.

Virgil, who understood everything without the need for explanations, launched in. 'Don't let your fear get the better of you. He may try to threaten us, but he won't be able to stop us from getting across this bridge.'

Then he turned to the plumped-up beast. 'Quiet now, you greedy wolf! I hope you choke on your gibes. We have good reason for our journey to the dark depths of Hell. Blessed ladies have set us on this path so don't make mischief. Remember that Satan and the other rebel angels were punished for trying to subvert God's authority. Nothing in the Kingdom of Hell can alter our course.'

Pluto understood these words meant he could not exercise any power over us. The cruel beast sank back in on himself, deflating as rapidly as a popped balloon.

The money-grubbing and wasteful

The next valley, stretching out before us in this store of evil, was filled with ever greater pain and suffering. I find it hard to put what I saw into words. If we weren't so easily led astray to do bad things, this misery wouldn't have to be endured. Here were the souls who had been obsessed with accumulating wealth for themselves as well as those who cared not a jot about passing it on, frittering all their wealth away.

Crowds of grimacing souls were organised in lines extending right round the rim of the abyss. With all the might they could muster in their chests, shoulders and arms, the first group was obliged to roll huge, heavy boulders in one direction while a second group rolled their boulders in the opposite direction. The two groups converged as though they were dancing a sort of hokey cokey, but they were dancing to tears rather than music. When they completed a full circle, they immediately turned around and headed back on their laden journeys the way they had come. One side shouted at the other, 'Why do you hold on to your riches?' The other side retorted, 'Why do you fritter your riches away?'

The weary souls puffed and panted as they retraced their tracks in the opposite direction. When they met again on the other side of the dreary circle, they rebuked each other just as before, and so the cycle repeated like wheels moving in contrary motion inside a clock. Back and forth, back and forth, all day and all night long.

These souls were both the instruments and the bearers of their own pain, and I was deeply disturbed by their inescapable turns of torture. I asked Virgil to tell me who they were, and he explained, 'Their minds were so blind in life that they had no sense of moderation in how to manage their wealth and possessions. You won't recognise anyone here. They have been so muddied by their inability to judge either generosity or prudence that their features have dissolved in the murk. Among them you will find the selfish, money obsessed Harpagon and Ebenezer Scrooge on the one side, and the careless squanderers, Lily Bart and Jay Gatsby of The Great Gatsby fame, on the other. They will collide and call out for eternity and when they are reunited with their bodies at the end of time, one half will have clenched fists for all the wealth they desperately held onto, and the other will be left with not so much as a hair on their head. Excessive hoarding and excessive spending have robbed them of Paradise and landed them in this mess. See it for what it is. No words can embellish it. You have seen what a mockery Fate makes of the desire for wealth and riches which sets people against each other. All the gold under the moon now, in the future, or ever before would not give rest to a single one of these weary souls.'

Fate

I was curious to learn more about Fate which Virgil had just mentioned. What was this essence which determines whether people fall on luck or hard times?

'You know,' Virgil said, 'people don't realise what small cogs they are in the context of the universe. Certainly, the role of Fate in people's lives is difficult to comprehend. It all started when God gave light to each minister in Heaven so that they could share wisdom. He also distributed riches equally on earth. God then ordained Fate as a general minister and guide for the world. Fate's role is to transfer riches on earth from person to person and from nation to nation as and when she deems necessary. Fate's power is untouchable by the human race and so, according to her whim, one country may see its wealth increase while another is struck by plague or economic crises. She can see into the future and pass judgement, and she carries out her reign just like other gods. She may change her mind at an instant and we see that in our daily lives as fame or success come and go in a flash. She deals us our fate like a pack of cards. Ironically, it may be better to be on the receiving end of bad luck in life as that is more likely to teach people the value of having faith in things which are constant, such as eternal life as a reward for a good life. As a divine minister, Fate is above the fray, immune to praise from those who enjoy the ups and deaf to the blame from those who experience the downs. She happily turns the wheel of fortune irrespective of its impact on our lives. If only we could rise above our humanity, we would do well to concern ourselves less with the vagaries of our earthly status. Now we need to continue our path down through Hell and witness even greater sorrow. It is already close to midnight and we can't allow ourselves to linger longer here.'

The Stygian marsh: the angry, proud and sullen

We crossed the circle to the far bank near a bubbling, boiling stream which cut through the rock and flowed into a channel. The water was pitch black. We followed the foul torrent down the spooky steps. At the bottom of the rocky slope, the murky stream met a marsh called Styx.

My attention was drawn to the scene in the bog below us. Naked figures coated in mud seemed to writhe in rage. They struck each other, not just with their fists but with their heads, chest and feet. They ripped flesh off each other with their teeth, piece by piece.

My attentive guide answered the questions in my mind. 'My son, here you can see the souls of those who succumbed to anger and fits of rage. You will also witness punishment for another sort of anger, the brooding one which bubbles up within people without ever finding release. Those are the sullen souls and, believe it or not, they are suffocating under the muddy water. If you look closely, you can see bubbles of air rising to the surface betraying their brooding existence.'

The "stuck-in-the-muds" gurgled through their throats, unable to formulate clear words. 'We were sullen in life despite the joys of nature and the sun's rays. We kept our anger fuming inside our hearts and now we bubble out our rage in the boggy waters.'

We circled round the stinking marsh between the dry bank and the mire of the pond, looking down on the souls drowning in the mud below, until at last we reached the foot of a tall tower.

CANTO 8

Angry, Proud and Sullen; the River Styx

Submerged in the Stinking River Styx

When they reach the City of Discord, our two travellers have arrived at the lower part of Hell. The nature of sin changes here, from the sins of human weakness in the circles above to those of conscious acts of evil. The line crossed is from sins of the flesh to sins of the intellect. These are much more serious because they are premeditated.

Crossing the river Styx; Phlegyas

On the approach to the tower, we had noticed two small lights flickering like flames at the top of the tallest turret. I assumed they were designed to help travellers find their location in the murky fog, rather like a lighthouse warns sailors of rocks and signals land. In fact, it turned out that they acted as an alert, signalling our arrival to the surrounding neighbourhoods. This became clear when a third flame flickered in response some way into the distance.

I asked Virgil to explain what the signals were for and he said, 'Look carefully through the mist across the muddy water and you should see who and what the signal is actually for.'

No sooner had he said these words than a little boat pinged across the water as fast as a hare from a trap. A lone boatman stood at the helm and shouted out, 'Ha, now I have you within my grasp, wretched soul!'

Not for the first time, Virgil intervened. 'Phlegyas, Phlegyas, put a sock in it! You have the wrong end of the stick. You are required to simply ferry us across the marsh. Do not mistake us for angry or sullen souls who have escaped from the sickly slurry of the fifth circle.' Phlegyas fumed like someone who has been tricked and grumbled at the deception.

My trusted guide stepped onto the boat and put his hand out for me to follow suit. No sooner had I boarded than the boat sank deeply in the water, burdened by my bodyweight, and I became aware of the difference between me and the souls who were like wisps of air. The ancient vessel turned and moved away from the bank, ploughing its way under the new burden.

Tybalt Capulet

We journeyed across the stagnant water and were midway across when the boat was suddenly rocked by a jolt from beneath. A soul steeped in mud drew himself up to the surface and called, 'What do you think you are doing here before your time is up?'

I was taken aback by the arrogance of this filthy, raging soul but maintained my composure. 'I am not a sinner like you but am passing through this dark void. Your stink-covered face makes for a good disguise, but tell me why you are so bold as to approach me? Who are you?'

Virgil put his hand on my shoulder to steady me, and also the boat, which was tipping as I leant in to inspect the cocky voice. 'That angry ruffian is Tybalt Capulet, made famous by William Shakespeare in his tragedy, Romeo and Juliet. You have already met Juliet amongst the lustful souls. This is her cousin who couldn't contain his rage and was constantly picking fights with people who opposed him.'

The soul was now livid that his identity had been revealed. His hands reached up onto the boat's rim, intending to capsize us, but Virgil was quick to head off any harm and pushed the offending soul away. My feathers were ruffled by his brazen and bolshie behaviour and I roared, 'Your destiny is here among the other tempestuous souls, so get yourself back in your filthy cage, dog!'

Virgil was impressed with my defiant response. He wrapped his arms around my neck and kissed my face saying, 'Good on you, my son! You did well to reproach him. Loyalty to his family alone would have been a good trait, but that very loyalty drove him to excessive rages and aggression, and he continues to let off the fumes of his temper rolling around like a pig in this mire. Let him drown in this soup!'

Shortly after the contretemps with Tybalt, I looked back to see a gang of muddy blobs attack him. Fists flew feistily. Blows and punches pummelled his slippery body as the angry souls shouted in unison, 'Down with Tybalt!'

With that, his body slunk back down into the filth, bubbles fizzing up in fury.

The City of Discord

We left that army of souls to their rampant rages only to encounter an army of a different sort. All of a sudden, I was startled by desperate cries, and I strained my eyes to see what further sorrow lay ahead. Virgil filled me in. 'We are now approaching the City of Discord. There we will find a population of sorrowful souls who are governed by an army of demons.'

I could make out a series of mosques rising from the valley beyond. A fire blazed within the city walls, lighting up the buildings like red, glowing embers. The confidence I had just displayed melted at once, and terror took its place. It took some time to reach the defensive moats which surrounded the miserable grey city of iron, but eventually the boatman drew in his oars and yelled, 'Out you get. This is the entrance.'

Opposition by the demons and Virgil's defeat

At the gates of the city, I saw thousands of fallen angels expelled in disgrace from Heaven. The fearsome demons chorused accusingly, 'Who is this man that walks undead and yet he dares to pass through the kingdom of the dead?'

Wise Virgil raised his hand as an offering of peace and sent one of their demonic tribe to request a quiet word in private. The demons could barely hold back their contempt. 'You can come through our gates but not with him. He has no invitation to enter, and he is foolish to assume eligibility to cross the fortifications of the darkest part of Hell where reason is deliciously perverted. Let him retrace his foolish steps and try to make it out of here unguarded and unguided!'

You cannot begin to imagine my rising panic. I feared that I wouldn't be able to continue my journey, and now I wasn't even sure I wanted to. Would I ever return to the sweet land of the living? I pleaded with Virgil, 'You have given me the courage to get this far, and you have protected me from beasts, monsters and evil tongues more times than I can count on this journey. Don't leave me now! I am terrified! If we can't go any further, let's just quickly turn back the way we came together.'

Virgil remained quite unperturbed. 'Listen, there's no need to worry. You know that nobody can stop our passage because it has been blessed by Heaven above. Wait for me here a moment and trust me while I talk to this ragged bunch. There is no way I will leave you alone in the underworld.'

I did feel abandoned in that moment and I was convinced I might never see my gentle guide again. I couldn't overhear what was discussed, but the negotiation drew to a quick conclusion when the demons scurried inside their city walls, arguing amongst each other. They slammed the gates in Virgil's face, leaving him on the threshold outside.

He slowly made his way back to me with his eyes downcast, and, for the first time, I saw disappointment and confusion on his face. He sighed, 'Who has dared to deny me access to the realm of pain below?' Then, turning to me, he said, 'I won't pretend that I'm not concerned by this turn of events, but we mustn't give up. I will not be thwarted whatever pranks they are up to in there to try to stop us. Their insolence is nothing new. They have tried before to block the entrance gate to Hell when the Mighty One visited here, but he broke that gate down and it remains wide open. Do you remember seeing the inscription for the dead above those gates? Ah, at last! Look, help is coming from above. He is treading a path round the circles of the abyss with no need for a guide. Divine Grace is sure to open the way for us to the City of Discord.'

CANTO 9

The Entrance to Lower Hell

Now the travellers arrive at the sixth circle which sits at the edge of the lower part of Hell where sins are calculated and wilful. Dante and Virgil meet the Furies whose job is to punish the moral crimes of humans. They frustrate the journey to salvation and create a prolonged moment of tension before the travellers broach the lower part of Hell.

In this circle, Dante meets sinners who have held harmful religious or cultural beliefs. They are set in their ways and adhere stubbornly to a principle which is misguided and causes harm to others. Virgil and Dante step to the right rather than the usual left to emphasise this intellectual perversion.

Dante's fear

My guide saw despair and terror written on my face, and my weakness seemed to spur him into taking responsibility. He instantly perked up and assumed control in an attempt to reassure me that all would be well. He drew breath for a moment and, as there was nothing to be seen in that black air and thick fog, listened out for a sign that help was indeed approaching.

Virgil voiced his concerns in a sort of mutter to himself, 'Look, I wasn't expecting those demons to stubbornly block our path, but I am sure that we will find a way through. Our journey has been authorised by a superior power to these malevolent beasts, so I am not sure what has gone wrong. If, as it seems, we need additional help to send the demons scattering, then why is it taking so long?'

The uncertainty which leaked through his show of confidence gave me little solace and I began to doubt that he knew his way through Hell as he had claimed. I tried to dig a little. 'When does it ever happen that a soul residing in Limbo, where the only punishment is the lack of hope of redemption, comes as far as this pitiful part of Hell?'

'Well, it doesn't happen often, but I have been to the very bottom of Hell once before. It was not long after I had died, and my soul had been removed to Limbo. A cruel witch made it her mission to reconcile certain souls with their bodies and she commanded me to fetch a soul from the deepest, darkest part of Hell, a region called Giudecca. Don't worry, I know the path well.'

The Furies and Medusa

He carried on talking, but my attention trailed off when I noticed a scuffle of what looked like bat wings at the top of the fiery tower. The scuffle turned to screeching, and three hellish blood-stained Furies rose up in the air. They were all the more terrifying as vivid green snakes coiled around their female forms. The top of their heads spewed forth a mass of tiny snakes with horns, all writhing around their terrifying temples. Virgil had no trouble identifying these wicked creatures as the slaves of Queen Proserpine, the queen of eternal suffering. He pointed out each fierce Fury in turn. There was Megaera on the left with a dagger in her belt, Alecto on the right with a flaming torch and the one in the middle was Tisiphone with a pitchfork at her feet.

The Furies beat their breasts and started tearing at themselves with their nails. They were screeching so loudly that I pulled myself closer to Virgil for comfort. Megaera squawked, 'Call for Medusa so we can turn them to stone! We let Theseus get away, but if we had turned him to stone then no more ugly mortals would dare to venture into our kingdom! Let's not miss the opportunity this time!' I had heard how Theseus had been freed from prison by Hercules having come to the underworld in an attempt to kidnap Proserpine. These Furies were clearly out for revenge.

I was remembering Theseus's story when Virgil cried out in urgency, 'Turn yourself around and shut your eyes because if Medusa appears and you look at her, you will never get out of here.' He either didn't trust his words to call me to action, or he feared I was too shocked to move, so he took it upon himself to turn me around and covered my eyes with his hands.

The divine messenger

A terrifying crash battered our ears, and the entire marsh of angry souls now roared with rage. We could hear the swell of huge waves pounding the shore. It sounded like a howling hurricane which might rip up trees and buildings, causing chaos and destruction in its wake.

Virgil removed his hands from my eyes and invited me to look beyond the foaming waves through the thick mist. Like terrified fish darting to the safety of the riverbed at an enemy approach, thousands of damned souls scurried away in fright at the sight of a giant foot which crossed the river Styx in a single step. The immense figure seemed to glide towards us effortlessly, occasionally swatting the thick air away from his face, as though in irritation.

Make no mistake, this was a being sent from the heavens above and his presence commanded deep respect. Virgil raised his finger to his lips to signal silence and I watched with awe. As the angel approached the city gate, the earth shook deeply with each step. He lifted a short wand and opened the gate without any resistance. As he stepped onto the dreaded threshold, disdain rang out, 'Despicable demons, you have been shut out of Heaven. What right do you have to display such arrogance? Why do you resist divine instruction? You know you will be punished more for every act of rebellion. What is the point of putting two fingers up at Fate? Just think of the livid scars that devilish Cerberus has on his chin and throat from God's chains for trying to stop Hercules from entering Hell!'

With that, he turned to go without so much as a glance in our direction. His mind seemed set on higher things again. Buoyed and protected by those heavenly words, we made our way towards the City of Discord with renewed confidence.

The burning tombs

Virgil and I passed through the gates unopposed this time. Eager to see what lay within the sealed fortress, I decided to take a good look around. In every direction were crowds of souls haunted with pain and suffering. Too many tombs lay scattered in this overburdened cemetery. The stone-filled plain resembled the Roman ruins at Glanum near St Rémy in France, but these were far more cruelly governed. Red hot flames licked the sides of the stone chambers, flickering across the edges like snakes' tongues eager to consume what lay within. Swarming above the tombs were small pieces of human flesh, and squabbling magpies fought for space on the frigid grey rims. The lids of the tombs were flung open and, from deep within, you could hear such tortured cries that they could only belong to miserable tormented souls.

I asked Virgil who these terrible sighing souls were, and he replied, 'They belong to souls whose religious beliefs led to unforgivable violence which destroyed lives. Here you will see perpetrators of female genital mutilation, forced marriages and normal sexual pleasure in their communities, and their unfeeling, stubborn beliefs are as hard as the slabs of slate that surround them. They are tormented by hell fire, sliced female genitalia and magpies to remind them of the scars they have caused, the happiness they have denied and the children they have wiped from existence.'

This time we set off to the right and made our way between the burning souls and the high walls of Discord.

CANTO 10

Believers in Harmful Practices

Tormented in Burning Tombs
by Genitalia and Magpies

These souls have turned their backs on a set of beliefs designed to build a world of hope and happiness. They are as good as dead to a world of tolerance and mutual respect and are entombed in unyielding stone coffins. The souls' tongues have been ripped out as they were the instrument used to instruct others to do harm. The voices we hear are those of the victims themselves. In the case of FGM victims, they speak through the mouthpiece of their excised flesh which has been cast from their bodies in life. Magpies speak for other victims whose lives have been manipulated in the name of honour or virtue.

We proceeded along a narrow path, my guide in front and me following behind. 'I am curious to see some of these souls lying in their tombs. The lids have all been taken off and nobody is watching over them, so surely there'll be no trouble if we stay a while?'

Virgil explained, 'The tombs will all be sealed when the souls return on Judgement Day with the bodies they left up on earth. You shouldn't expect to learn anything from these souls as they have lost their tongues and are unable to speak. The tongue was the instrument they used to give instructions for the awful violence caused to their victims: often their own children or children of family members. In death, their tongues have been ripped out. These first tombs contain the perpetrators of female genital mutilation, and the bloody pieces of flesh that you see swirling above the tombs are the thousands of excised female genitals. They are the mouthpiece for the victims' voices whose stories you will hear.'

Victim of female genital mutilation

Out of the blue, a voice came to me from a flying piece of flesh which hovered persistently over a nearby tomb. 'I recognise your accent and live in Italy near Rome. My body is living still but I speak through the flesh that was cruelly cut away, and my destiny is to torment my mother, lying here, who caused me untold pain. I was born in Sierra Leone where I lived with my mother and sister. When I was a little girl of eight years old, my mother told me I was going to have a party. She bought me a pretty green dress and invited a bunch of women to the festivities. There was music and dancing, and I was buzzing with happiness. Later, a group of four women, along with my mother, took me into an empty room. One of the women pinned me to the floor. Two others held each of my legs and, panicking, I tried to wriggle free. I started screaming when my mother left the room and an ugly old woman sat between my opened legs and took out a blade from a ragged piece of black cloth. The women held me down tight and this ugly hag proceeded to cut me. The pain was excruciating but the cutting didn't stop until I fainted. Afterwards my mother told me my husband would be able to love me when I grew up and I would be able to have children safely.

'After that day, I barely drank any water because weeing was so painful, my monthly bleeds were agonising. Later, when I married, my husband forced me to sleep with him, but it always hurt, and he eventually left me saying I had brought him bad luck. I have withheld my story for so long and I pray that you will spread the word when you return to the world above so that other victims may be spared such torture.'

The fluttering flesh rested on the edge of the tomb, exhausted from pain. Simultaneously, cries from the tomb escalated, and magpies converged on the mother's soul who was burning inside, pecking away at her eyes and feasting on their carrion. This was a strange story to my ears, but I moved on, reflecting deeply at the hurt in that heart.

Victim of forced marriage

At another tomb, I stopped in my tracks at the sound of a magpie calling out in a human voice, 'Is it true what I have heard? Are you hoping to return to the sweet life above? Please stop a moment to hear my story so that you may carry it back with you to tell the world. So many women from my culture have suffered subjugation, servitude and unhappiness just like me, but leaders in government need to take more action. There are many families like mine in India where the girl is treated like a piece of property. She is owned first by her parents and then by her husband. Her purpose is to cook, clean, run errands and bear children. My parents were themselves committed to an arranged marriage. They only met each other a week before they were married, and I have never seen them hug or even hold hands. I was bullied at school as I was the only Asian child in my class and I was sexually abused by a much older Asian man, a friend of the family. Unlike my brothers who went to university and could go out on dates, I dropped out of school and was told that I wouldn't be going to university. I was groomed and beaten by the same older man and was sent to India at the age of nineteen to be exorcised in an attempt to cleanse me of my "damage". My parents then started to search for a husband for me in India. I repeatedly refused these matches.

'I was brought back home to England and tried to escape my family by running away to a children's shelter. I slit my wrists as I wanted to end the hell I was living on earth. I was hospitalised and my parents started a new search for a husband. The negotiating families eventually settled on a pairing, although at no point did I give my consent to the marriage. However, he seemed kind enough and, to begin with, I wasn't worried. However, after our wedding he started to abuse me. He'd pin me down and perform violent sex. I found it agony. His mother demanded more and more dowry from my parents, but they couldn't afford the thousands of pounds requested, and I was punished. I was made to rise before dawn to clean the house, my meals were monitored, and I could never leave the house. If his mother was disappointed with my work, I would suffer beatings. It got so bad that finally I collapsed and was taken to hospital. Only then did my parents intervene. I started divorce proceedings and then I could rebuild my life.'

She fell silent, but I hope that her words, which I have faithfully recorded, stir future generations to change attitudes and protect young women from harmful relationships.

Victim of honour-based violence

Shortly after this encounter, a flock of magpies landed at our feet, blood dripping from their beaks as they paused their feast of a pitiful tormented soul. I asked what stubborn soul it was that they were destined to damage, and the central bird, the largest of the three, told me that the birds on this side of the sixth circle were the mouthpieces for women who were victims of honour-based violence. They were not speaking for murdered victims as those who killed in the name of honour were allocated further down in the depths of Hell, in the seventh circle. The magpie was keen for me to hear her story and I listened intently.

I had seen honour-based violence on numerous occasions in my life. I knew of many men who battled in duels to assert their honour. A verbal or physical slight was often settled with a fight in open pasture or forest clearings, earning honour for the winner. In many cases, women were the victims of honour-based violence. Feuding families were very protective of their womenfolk, and if one should stray into the arms of an enemy family, she would be hounded out by her own flesh and blood. I knew that some cultures saw their women as reproductive powers which belonged to the family. If that power was uncontrolled, then it was a huge slight on the family's honour and murder was a common response. Not long before this journey began, I read an account of a man in Syracuse in Sicily who paraded through the streets with his sister's blood on his clothes. He had slaughtered her for her alleged misdemeanours and believed this would increase his honour in the eyes of the world.

The magpie started, 'I come from a loving Indian family living in France. I had a happy childhood and enjoyed my time at school. My parents taught me right from wrong and we had a loving relationship. However, things changed when I was seventeen. I met a boy who made me laugh and I felt so happy with him that I started meeting him after school. I enjoyed experimenting with make-up and wore small tops and skirts like my western friends but when my parents found out, they stopped me from going out and locked me in my room before and after school. They escorted me to and from the school gates so that I couldn't meet him on my own. They beat me if they suspected I had spent time with him at school. This carried on for twelve months until I told my school, and my teachers informed the authorities. After that I used to lie to people, pretending that I had a different, more normal life that wasn't the sad insular one I was now finding it so hard to break out of. I used to pretend I was going on holiday with my family but actually I would shut myself away for weeks on end. I am still coming to terms with what freedom really is. Please carry my story back to earth to make doctors, law enforcers and judges more acutely aware of the effects of abuse perpetrated in the name of honour.'

These words affected me profoundly. My own father's cousin, Geri, had been killed by a member of the Sachetti family in a vengeful murder driven by the idea of family honour. Unlike many of my contemporaries, I believe that private honour killings are inexcusable. Society should develop new laws and codes of practice to ensure peaceful and harmonious living. I hope that my words will set a path for change.

As I reflected on the future for societies across the world, I marvelled at the stories I was hearing from souls ranging from the distant past to the distant future. There was so much to learn from history and yet, here was evidence that history and people's actions so often repeated themselves. While some of the tales from the future involved unfamiliar elements, I recognised the passions that drove the miserable sinners to commit their immoral acts. I then wondered what these damned souls could see of the future given they shared the destinies of souls from all ages. I asked Virgil to tell me more.

'Hell's victims can indeed see things in the future albeit indistinctly. After death, the soul sees all things with the light of truth. Their knowledge of the present is the weakest and so you may be asked to relay news from the living world. However, all knowledge will die as soon as Judgement Day closes its doors on the future.'

He then beckoned me on to follow him.

The Organisation and Layout of Hell

In this canto, Dante explains the layout of Hell as largely based on the philosopher Aristotle's classifications of sin. Upper Hell contains sinners of incontinence who have fallen to temptations of the flesh such as lust, greed and anger. Either side of Upper Hell are the sinners in Limbo who have no faith and those who hold harmful beliefs. In Lower Hell there are the sinners of malice, people who have made a conscious decision to commit a crime against friends, family or other members of society. These are more serious sins because they involve reason, God's special gift to mankind, to offend others and, to Dante's particular regret, to break the bonds of society.

Dante's anxiety

I remined silent as I tried to digest Virgil's words, thinking about my own future. I thought back to Ciacco's prophesy of my exile from Florence and felt weakened by an impending loss of power to make a difference to my people. I was saddened by a sense of impending exclusion from a place and people that meant so much to me.

Virgil could see that I was unsettled in my thoughts and, as we were walking, he asked, 'What's upsetting you?'

I opened up to him. He quickly offered me some wise words and, pointing his finger firmly towards me, said, 'Remember what you have heard about your future and listen to me carefully. It won't be long before you see the sweet rays of Beatrice who embodies all things blessed, and then you will understand your life's journey. You will be certainly able to make a difference to society by recording these tales from our journey.'

Virgil then turned to the left, away from those dreadful city walls and we headed towards the centre of the abyss, following a path over to the next valley. Even at a distance we retched at the stink.

Organisation and distribution of the damned souls in Hell

We came to the edge of a cliff, ringed with huge broken boulders above an even crueller crowded pit. Utterly overwhelmed by the stench thrown up by the deep abyss, we had to step back from the edge.

Virgil said, 'We need to stay here a bit longer until we have acclimatised to the vile air. Then it won't bother us anymore.'

I asked if he could think of a constructive way to make up for the lost time, but he was already on the case.

'My son, we are about to enter the lower part of Hell, three circles just like the ones we have left behind. They sit within the very same cliffs and they get narrower as you approach the bottom. They are full of miserable souls but, to speed up the next part of our journey, I will put time aside now to explain how sins are allocated within this pitiful pit.

'Every sin that a person chooses to commit angers God because it ends with injury. Whether the sin is one of violence or fraud, it is bound to harm other people. To commit fraud, a person uses considerable thought and pre-meditation; they are misusing God's gift to mankind of reason. This perversion of nature really angers God, so the fraudulent souls are placed in the deepest part of Hell and they suffer the most pain.

'The first circle of Lower Hell, which is the seventh in the whole of Hell, is full of violent souls. Violence can involve grievous bodily harm, rape, and murder, even mass murder. Each form of violence has its own ditch. The first ditch contains souls who have seriously wounded other people with intent, including injury through fire or torture. The second ditch contains the souls of rapists. They have violently taken control of someone else's body for sexual pleasure without consent. Finally, there are the murderers and mass murderers who have robbed people of their lives. They may be motivated by a warped addiction or an impulse to fulfil a personal, political, religious or cultural strategy for dominance.

'Fraud is a disease of conscience, perpetrated against trusted friends, family or total strangers. Fraud destroys the bonds that tie people together, and so the second circle of Lower Hell, which is the eighth in the whole of Hell, holds in its claws: cheats, blackmailers, human traffickers, child abductors and money launderers. You will also find people in public offices like governments and the church who abuse their positions for material gain, breaking the trust and respect they should earn from the people they serve.

'Fraud committed against people you know, or where there is an existing bond of love and kindness, is even worse. These souls have broken a special relationship and have committed the worst of all sins. The ninth circle, the smallest in Hell, sits at the centre of the universe under Satan's throne. It entraps all traitors and entombs them in ice.'

I was hungry for more answers, so I asked, 'Virgil, your guidance is making everything so much clearer to me, but I have another question. I have understood the sorts of sins which are punished below us here, but what about the souls we saw before we reached Discord? The ones who were beaten by the rain, hurled by the wind, stuck in the mud, insulted and torn apart? Why aren't they punished within the burning walls of Discord? And if they haven't angered God, then why do they suffer so much pain?'

Virgil was quick to respond, 'You must be aware by now that sins have varying degrees of gravity. The sins we are about to see are the product of free choice and premeditation. In contrast, the sins we saw above stem from an excess of passion, a weakness of the flesh supplanting reason. They are not a conscious attempt to harm others. They are sins of incontinence and attract less punishment as they offend God less. If you think about the sorts of sinners we saw outside Discord, it should be clear why they are separate from these more wicked souls within the city walls, and why divine wrath strikes them less hard.'

Just as the sun chases away the shadows of the night, I felt as though scales had fallen from my eyes. I was grateful to be taught in such a clear and concise way. I understood so much more about the nature of the different sins, and I felt ready to tackle the next stage of our journey.

'Come on now. It's time to follow me again,' Virgil said. 'Let's go quickly as it will soon be dawn. Just a little further to go. Then we'll start to climb down the cliff.'

Perpetrators of GBH

Tormented by Raining Fire on Burning Sand

The first ring of the seventh circle contains the souls who have committed grievous bodily harm. Virgil explains the landslide which marks their route into the circle of the violent souls. Dante reflects on the question of greatness in life and the divergence between human values and divine values which ultimately dictate souls' fates.

The landslide and the Minotaur

The spot where we were to make our way down the bank looked pretty unappealing. The cliff edge was a landslide where rocks had tumbled dangerously down the slope to the ditch below, but it did open up a rocky route down. It was not only the path ahead which looked treacherous; if you had seen the creature that had made its outpost there, you would be forgiven for thinking it would be better to turn back.

There, right on the cliff edge, I saw a monster, the shame of Crete, poised in a threatening pose. This beast was the fearsome Minotaur, and you may be familiar with his story. King Minos's wife, Pasiphae, fell in love with a bull, so she dressed up as a cow in the hope of raising her appeal. The disguise was a success. They conceived this Minotaur together. He was half-human, half-bull and, I now remembered, he had an unquenchable appetite for humans. As soon as he saw us, he opened his jaws and bellowed before biting himself, consumed with frustrated rage.

Virgil raised his voice and taunted the beast, 'Are you afraid that your killer, Theseus, has returned to finish you off a second time? Make way for us. This man is not Theseus. He has not arrived here thanks to the clues of the spiders' webs that your sister, Ariadne, once laid in the maze so Theseus could find you. No, this man is here to see your pain and suffering.'

At these words, the Minotaur reeled and rampaged like a bull who has been dealt a mortal blow but then breaks free from his chain and staggers about in a crazy fury. Virgil took his chance and shouted, 'Run! Make for the path! Let's get past him while he is blindly raging.'

We made our way down, slipping and sliding on the craggy surface which shifted about under our feet. I was thinking about what we had just seen when Virgil said, 'You are probably wondering about this landslide and how it has come to be guarded by that angry beast. As I told you, I have descended through these parts of Hell once before, but this landslide wasn't here then. It was not long after that journey, if I remember rightly, when the Almighty One came to Discord to gather up all the non-Christian souls like me and remove us to Limbo. His coming made all the sides of this deep, vile abyss tremble so much that the ancient rocks crumbled and caused the landslide whose devastation we see before us. At the time, we all said that the universe must be feeling love. We had been taught to believe that the universe was held together by a tension between order and disorder, between love and hate. If pure love alone was felt, then the universe would return to chaos and this is how it seemed at that moment.'

The desert of burning sand

Beyond the base of the fallen rocks, we came to a halt close to the edge of a sweeping desert plain. There was not a single living plant in sight and an intense heat radiated against our faces. The sand at our feet was packed hard and baked just like the vast Sahara, the perennial home of Bedouin nomads. Here, however, there was no life to behold. You will be shocked by the power of divine justice when you read about what I saw there!

Flocks of naked souls were crying miserably. Some were lying on the ground; others were sitting with their knees huddled up; and others were constantly walking about. Sheets of fire rained down steadily over the entire stretch of sand like snow in the mountains when there is no wind. I thought of the flames which fell on Alexander the Great's army in the hottest part of India when they crossed the desert. The great leader got his soldiers to stamp out the fire with their feet to stop it spreading. Here too, the heavenly-sent flames of rain landed on the souls but, as they landed on the sand, the ground caught fire like kindling, scorching the soles of their feet. Those miserable souls looked like they were beating drums as their hands twitched ceaselessly, fighting to brush off the fresh flames, now here, now there, burning their skin.

Aaron Burr

I noticed one particular soul standing unusually tall and proud. He remained strangely still as if totally unaffected by the raining fire. 'Virgil, you have given me answers to everything so far and have removed all the awful obstacles in our way, apart from the difficult demons who slammed their doors in our face at the City of Discord. Can you tell me who that proud soul is over there with a frown on his face looking scornful of his punishment?'

The soul realised that I was asking my guide about him and answered for himself, 'I have no regrets for the injury I inflicted on my political opponent, Alexander Hamilton, in our infamous duel. He brought death on himself. I simply gave him the injury he deserved when he thwarted my political ambitions time and again. I needed to show the United States of America that I was their man, not the accursed Hamilton.'

Virgil now turned on him directly. 'Burr, you are a fool. Your refusal to put your anger to bed brings you significantly more torment than the physical pain you are enduring. Jealousy of your rival's political success eats away at your heart and that, in itself, is a fitting punishment for your lack of respect.'

In a calmer voice, Virgil explained to me, 'This soul's pride and scorn are well-deserved fiery adornments branded on his chest. The opponent he fatally injured in a duel was an important politician and economist who laid the bedrock of the financial system of what became the mightiest economy on earth. This wretch was never to reach such greatness in his life and look where he has ended up now! Come on, I need you to follow me but keep to the edge where the rain doesn't fall.'

The Gladiator, Maximus

As we walked, Virgil pointed out the famous gladiator, Maximus, who fought many successful battles in the Colosseum at Rome. He told me that Maximus's ability to fight with a sword was unrivalled but that he famously stopped short of killing a fearful opponent, Tigris of Gaul, earning himself the sobriquet "Maximus the Merciful". I felt a certain admiration for his achievements and persistence in overcoming jealous enemies. As I understood it, the Emperor Aurelius even nominated him as his successor, causing the emperor's son, Commodus, untold jealousy. However, here was the once-proud gladiator, shrivelling into cinders: a reminder that human greatness on earth is powerless in the face of divine judgement.

Black Mamba

Another soul, sitting near the edge of the plain where we walked, drew her knees up to her chin. I asked her name and if she would tell me a bit about herself. She immediately looked distrustful, but I reassured her that I meant no harm. She said she was Black Mamba. Now it was my turn to become distrustful. Was she a lethal snake?

'I was created by Quentin Tarantino and my real name was Beatrix. My ex-lover, Bill, tried to kill me on my wedding day even though I was pregnant with his child. I spent four years in a coma. When I came out of the coma, I vowed to injure anybody who had played a part in robbing me of my life and that of my child. I secured a highly crafted sword from a legendary Japanese swordsmith to carry out my revenge. A skilled fighter, I may be, but now I am subjected to swords of falling fire which pierce my skin for eternity.'

Then she fell silent.

CANTO 13

Rapists

Transformed into Bushes in a Wood with Harpies Tearing at their Branches

Dante and Virgil migrate from the burning plain to the wood where rapists are punished. Just as the rapists took another person's body for their own pleasure, now they are deprived of their bodily form and instead have the form of wild thornbushes. Vicious bird-like Harpies tear at their leaves and break their branches in the same way that the rapists broke other people's bodies in committing their crimes.

Discussion about nihilism with Tyler Durden

We had almost completed a full circle of the burning plain when a soul who was lying under the falling fire tugged at my cloak. 'What brings you to this place of eternal suffering? Please take a moment to talk with me.'

I explained that I was only visiting the Kingdom of Hell and that I was on a journey of self-knowledge and redemption. I asked him what it was he wanted to share with me.

'I would like to know why you think looking at all the suffering souls in this wretched place will lead you to happiness and salvation? My name is Tyler Durden and if you ever make it back to the world above us then please remind people of my name as they may have heard of Chuck Palahniuk's story, Fight Club.'

'I have not heard of your name, but I can tell you that my visit is divinely willed and that is a good enough reason to justify its importance. I have already met with souls who are not Christian believers They are hanging suspended in Limbo. Whether you have faith or not, the consequences of human actions in life are here for all to see. If we can recognise what is bad within ourselves when we are still alive, then we can take a better path leading to happiness. I am afraid, you left it too late. This is your eternity.'

Tyler grimaced through his pain but challenged me further. 'I understand that I am here for the injuries I have inflicted, but I am resolute in my belief that people need to break out of the success or failure psyche by which we define ourselves. Instead, through the physical pain of fighting, we can chip away at the cocoon provided by society until we are reduced to the raw essence of ourselves. Forget striving to follow rules, or someone else's definition of good behaviour, or the "right path". We should make of ourselves what we want without externally imposed conditions.'

I understood Tyler's philosophy but saw that it was fatally flawed. 'You may not agree with the creed or the laws which society has laid down for you but, without a solid framework, the world would fall into anarchy. Happiness on earth is achieved through good government and well-enforced, sensible laws. When you were alive, you may not have cared much for your soul, but the torment to which you are now subjected must prove to you that there is a superior power, one previously missing from your life. It's a bit late for you to redeem yourself now, but I know that eternal happiness is not possible without faith and it is the church's role to guide us to salvation. You must see that the suffering you currently endure is nothing to do with reducing you to your raw essence, but everything to do with making you see the error of your ways. There is no reconstruction from where you are now!'

Virgil patted me lightly on the back, pleased with my discussion and nudged me onwards.

We left the burning plain behind us and crossed a small bridge to the second ring of this violent circle, arriving at the edge of a wood but with no sign of a path to direct us.

The leaves weren't green, but dark and brittle; the branches weren't smooth, but knotted and gnarled; there were no fruits growing, but thorns of poison. Even evil-loving wolves, bears and snakes avoided this inhospitable wasteland. Instead, we saw ugly Harpies who once drove the Trojans from the Strophades islands with their terrifying predictions of impending disaster, and now were making their nests in this withered wood. The Harpies had wide hawk wings but human necks and faces. Their feet were claws and their chests were covered with feathers. We heard their piercing shrieks hail down from the trees above our heads.

Virgil explained where we were, 'Before we go any further, I will tell you a little about our location. This is the second ring of the circle of violent souls and this wood extends all the way to the blood-filled river Phlegethon. Look carefully around you and you will see things which, if you simply heard it from me, you would just not believe.'

There was the sound of wailing voices all around me, but I couldn't work out who was making the terrible din. I felt totally bewildered and stopped suddenly in my tracks. I think he must have thought that I thought that the cries coming from the bushes belonged to souls who were hidden from view.

Almost as a joke, and to prove his point about needing to see to believe,

Virgil asked me to break off a piece of one of the bushes. 'When you snap off a piece of that branch, you will be snapped into realising you have completely the wrong idea.'

Artemisia Gentileschi's rape by Agostino Tassi

I put out my arm to break off a twig from a large thornbush and the piece in my hand shouted, 'Hey, why have you broken me?'

The twig oozed thick blood and cried out a second time, 'Why have you torn me? Have you no pity? Once we were human, but look, now we are bushes. If we had been the souls of poisonous snakes, your hand would have shown more mercy.'

I was reminded of fresher, greener logs which burn at one end and hiss at the other as trapped moisture is released in a cloud of steam. There was a frothing fizz as words and blood came spluttering out of the broken twig simultaneously. On an impulse, I dropped the twig and stood rooted to the spot, ashamed of what I had done.

Virgil attempted to offer an apology to the offended soul. 'If this man had been able to take me at my word rather than seek the proof, he wouldn't have laid a finger on you. I am sorry to say that your situation is so unbelievable that I felt he would only understand if he saw the evidence for himself. I am truly sorry. Now is your chance to tell your story, as he may put in a good word, if you deserve it, on his return to the world.'

The twig blew hard through one end to break the seal of dried blood and, as the breath pushed through, out came a voice. 'My name is Tassi and I am suffering punishment for my abuse of the artist Artemisia Gentileschi. Her father was a friend of mine and she was there for the taking as she assisted her father in his studio all day. It is true that I forced her into the bedroom, locked the door and pinned her to the bed. I shoved a gag in her mouth and penetrated her as she screamed and clawed at me. When I had finished with her, she leapt off the bed and grabbed a knife, but she was unable to inflict injury. I promised her I would marry her in order to make her honourable and, as she believed me, she allowed me to continue to bed her for months afterwards. I had no intention of marrying her and her father brought the case to court. Even after torture by the authorities who pulled and twisted her fingers to verify her account, she held that I had promised to marry her. Now I am paying for the violence I inflicted on her body. She has achieved the upper hand, however, as her powerfully evocative paintings have given her fame and glory.'

I asked him to explain how his soul came to be entangled in the gnarled bushes and if any soul had managed to free itself from the confines of the conifers. He explained, 'When the violent soul is uprooted from its body, Minos sends it to the seventh circle. It falls into the wood and germinates wherever fate happens to fling it. First, it grows into a sapling and then into a wild and thorny bush. The Harpies feast on our leaves, causing us terrible pain and as they shred us open, our pain is shrilly ventilated through our wounds. Like the other souls, we will see our bodies on Judgement Day, but we will not be able to climb back into our bodies as you can't get back something which you took from another person and that is only right. No, tragically, we will drag our bodies back to this dismal wood and we will hang them on the thorns of our evil souls.'

We expected the twig to say more but were suddenly startled by a commotion in the bushes nearby. I thought I could hear the hammering hooves and pig-like squeals of a wild boar being chased through the undergrowth by vicious dogs. In the blink of an eye, two souls came hurtling through the thorny branches with deep scratches all over their naked bodies.

The one in front cried out, 'Please, I beg you, put an end to this suffering!'

The second one retorted, 'Neptune, you shouldn't have taken Medusa from behind because if you had looked her in the eye, she would have turned you to stone, and you wouldn't be running for your life in these wretched woods!'

The speaker was Calypso. She was trailing behind Neptune and huddled up against a bush to catch her breath, but respite didn't last long. Bounding through the wood behind them was a pack of flame-eyed, drooling hounds of the night. They didn't hesitate to pounce on the crouching prize, digging in their teeth and tearing her from limb to limb.

The sheltering bush wept in vain through each bloody, broken wound. 'Calypso, why are you hiding under me? I had nothing to do with your shameful imprisonment of Ulysses on your island, Ogygia. You raped him and held him close to your chest, guarding him jealously for seven years. I will not guard you for as long! Gentle visitor, I was a Florentine like you. Please ease the pain of this excessive cruelty which has torn my leaves from me. Gather my broken leaves together and place them at my wretched roots!'

Murderers

Submerged in a River of Boiling Blood

The third ring in the circle of violent souls is home to murderers. The sinners boil in a river of blood and centaurs keep guard, shooting arrows at anyone attempting to escape. Dante meets mass murderers from the future and is shocked that the world seems set to continue on a path of hostility, destruction and division. He realises that the inescapable suffering to which the souls are subjected for eternity proves the fallibility of human decisions and their potentially lethal consequences.

The river Phlegethon and the centaurs

I was filled with pity for the unnamed soul from my hometown who had the additional torment of being savaged by those rampaging hounds. I gathered up the scattered leaves and gave them to the soul whose voice was growing faint.

We emerged from the wood and found ourselves next to a small stream. Picturing those blood-red bubbles makes me shudder even now. Virgil said, 'We will turn to the left and follow this stream, but look carefully at what lies ahead, because we are approaching the river where all those wretches who have committed murder boil in the blood they have spilled. I promise to tell you the story behind Hell's rivers once we have seen these stewing souls.'

Sometimes it is blind stupidity or anger of the moment that leads people to commit foolish acts of violence. At other times, the violence is intricately planned and designed, and, in that case, whole nations, cultures or religions may be under attack. Whether the action is of a moment or a lifetime, its consequences last forever and the proof was in the countless souls lying bathed in eternal suffering here.

Just as Virgil had warned, a wide river wound its way around the edge of the wood. Running alongside the banks I could see an army of centaurs, half-man, half-horse with quivers on their backs laden with arrows ready for the hunt. Seeing us come down the bank, they stopped running. Three of them broke off from the troop with bows and arrows at the ready. Then one of them, standing some way off, shouted, 'Stop where you are! What is your rightful place in this prison? Don't come any further or I'll draw my bow!'

Virgil was quick to assume authority. 'We will answer to your leader, Chiron, when we get closer. Impulsive violence never did you any good.'

Then he nudged me with the back of his hand and said, 'That is Nessus who fell in love with Hercules' wife, Deianira, and tried to rape her. Hercules injured him but Nessus gave Deianira his cloak soaked in poisoned blood, claiming that whoever wore it would fall in love with her. She gave the cloak to Hercules in an attempt to rebuild their relationship, but, when Hercules put on the fateful cloak, he became furious and died. The centaur in the middle, looking thoughtful and wise, is the impressively gifted Chiron who tutored both Achilles and Hercules in the art of war. The other one is Pholus, who met an unfortunate end when he accidentally dropped one of Hercules' poisoned arrows on his foot. Thousands of these centaurs patrol the river shooting arrows at any soul who dares to emerge from the boiling blood.'

We drew closer to the swift, agile beasts. Then Chiron took an arrow from the quiver on his back. With its tip, he parted his shaggy moustache to reveal his great mouth and said to his comrades, 'Have you noticed that the one at the back moves everything he touches? That doesn't happen with dead people.'

Virgil was standing close enough to Chiron to hear his comment and said, 'He is indeed alive, and he has been granted special permission to be shown the dark valley. Necessity brings him here rather than pleasure. Blessed Beatrice left the choirs of angels in Heaven to engage me in this extraordinary task. He is not a murderer and I am not his soul. As our journey has the backing of blessed power, please can you release one of your soldiers to be a guide for us? He can show us where to ford the river and also carry my companion across on his back as he is not a spirit who can float through the air.'

Chiron craned his neck to look at Nessus standing behind him and said, 'You are to guide them and if you come up against another troop, make sure they let you pass.'

Adolf Hitler and Osama bin Laden

We moved along the bank with our newly acquired escort, and I witnessed high pitched screams steaming up from the cooking flesh which stewed in the crimson broth boiling below our feet.

I saw souls submerged right up to their eyebrows and the great centaur said, 'These are mass murderers and terrorists who have caused the death of thousands of innocent people. They were driven by an obsession to eliminate a religion, culture or nation and now they are paying the price for their wickedness. The one with the black block of moustache poking out of the bloodbath is Adolf Hitler who, at a time in your future, will be responsible for a terrible genocide, killing millions of Jews and hoping to exterminate the entire Jewish population in Europe. Hitler and contemporary myth denounced the Jews for betraying Germany: the Jews were responsible for German military defeat in the First World War, leading to a left-of-centre government and sparking years of economic hardship. Hitler wanted to create a master race of blue-eyed, blond Aryans and saw the Jewish population as the antithesis to that. His Nuremberg Laws stripped Jews of their German citizenship, and you too will come to know how that feels as you will be banished from your hometown not long from now. Jews were forbidden to marry non-Jews; they were removed from schools, from the army and from their professions. Propaganda swept through Germany and Jews were publicly humiliated. As Hitler attacked and conquered Europe in the Second World War, he captured more and more Jews. His mission culminated with the Final Solution in which millions of Jews were carted off to gas chambers to be exterminated.'

I was horrified by the scale of such human slaughter and was deeply saddened to learn of two World Wars which would cause further bloodshed and loss of life. Things were bad enough in the life that I knew in Italy with cities and political parties constantly at each other's throats in the fight for supremacy. The prophecy of my exile also filled me with dread, and I turned to Virgil. 'I will write down all the things I am learning, including the news about my exile. This is not the first time I have heard that sorry news, but if I manage to reach Beatrice who knows everything, I hope she will shed light on it all. Let the wheel of fortune turn. Whatever my future holds, I am ready for it.'

Nessus pointed out another submerged soul whose wriggling body was sending out waves. I could just about make out a white coloured head cloth sticking out above the bloody surface, but it had already absorbed a good deal of bubbling blood and was slowly turning red.

'That is Osama bin Laden who will orchestrate terrorist attacks on America including the twin towers in New York in the name of the Islamic extremist group called Al-Qaeda. The attacks were planned as an act of retaliation against America, democracy, Christianity, Judaism and the West. Parts of the Muslim world were irritated by America's support for Israel and they felt American presence in the central Arab states threatened unwelcome colonisation. You will find this hard to imagine, but Al-Qaeda terrorists hijacked four flying vessels carrying human passengers, and two of them were directed at twin towers built over a thousand feet tall. The towers contained one hundred and ten floors used by business outfits. The passengers trapped in the flying vessels, called planes, died instantly. The towers were razed to the ground by the impact which caused a huge explosion of fire. These attacks killed almost three thousand people and the story travelled instantly round the world. Osama bin Laden was tracked down and killed by American forces in Pakistan, a Muslim-majority country located in southern Asia, home to Gupta, Rajput and Mughal Empires.'

When Nessus had finished speaking, the wretched soul wriggled so violently that his whole head was sucked under the stewing blood. The surface settled for a moment. Then turbulence returned as the soul hauled himself up to see who had betrayed his identity. No sooner had his nose protruded from the broth than a series of arrows hailed down on the soul's head from our centaur's bow and his cries were swallowed up by the hot pot that was now his eternal home.

This story of religious divisions, war and terror landed heavily in my ears. I remain terrified for the future, but I hope that my testimony of human evil and evidence of divine retribution will put an end to violence and make a place for peace on earth.

CANTO 15

The River Phlegethon

River of Boiling Blood

Nessus points out serial killers and murderers and Dante understands how people can show two very different faces: one familiar and predictable and the other utterly warped. He recognises two military generals from his home town of Florence. Closer to home, Dante learns of the reasons for Florence's moral and political decline. He blames desire for material wealth and the rise to power of the bourgeois community for the corruption in individuals, families and society. However, there are often two sides to the story. Even here, we see the contrast between greatness and fame achieved by people on earth, and the ugly horror of Divine Judgement in Hell, which effectively undermines their life's achievements.

Dennis Nilsen and Myra Hindley

A little further on, the centaur stopped over some souls, boiled in blood up to their throats. He pointed out one adrift from the others. 'That is Dennis Nilsen, who attacked and killed at least fifteen young men and found himself behind bars for life. I am afraid his story is particularly gruesome. He usually strangled or drowned them before sexually abusing their flaccid bodies. When he was finished with them, he would hide the bodies under the floorboards or chop them up and flush them away like sewage. One of his victim's heads was found in a stewing pot having been severed and boiled. He preyed on vulnerable, often homeless boys but, to the world, he seemed a normal citizen. He worked in the police, keeping peace on the streets, and then he helped unskilled people find employment. He was even promoted for his efforts. Look how he has fallen now!'

Not for the first time, my attention was caught by an appeal from a suffering soul to stop. This time, a female voice called to me, 'See how I am suffering for having robbed people of their lives. I need you to know the whole story and to carry it back to the people who are still alive.'

I said that I would hear her out although I was sure I would feel no sympathy for her plight.

She took up her story. 'I had a difficult childhood with a father who drank too much and encouraged me to retaliate against the boys who picked fights with me at school. If I didn't fight my corner at school, then he would beat me for being a weakling. I became fascinated with one boyfriend, partly because he had already been jailed for theft before he was eighteen. He became a notorious murderer and my companion in crime. He is also in this hot bath of blood. I am grateful for small mercies but, thankfully, he is boiling at a safe distance. He was manipulative and threatening but I was obsessed with him. I needed his protection and yet I couldn't escape even if I'd tried. He would drug, rape and beat me if I made him jealous or unhappy. I killed to please him as I believed that was the way to make him treat me well. Together, we killed five children and buried them all over the windswept moors around Manchester in England. It was like a game of hide and seek, us against the authorities, but no one is laughing now. I have damaged the lives of both the dead and their loved ones who were left living. I was judged once on earth, but now my pain and suffering are eternal vengeance for those crimes.'

Passionfruit

Then I saw a group of souls who had their head and shoulders above the bloody river's surface, and I recognised quite a few of them. I asked Nessus to tell me about one I didn't recognise. He had a round head and dark skin, and he wore a strong helmet with a grid of metal bars in front of his face and a chinstrap.

Nessus saw me looking confused at this strange helmet and explained, 'That headgear is worn by sportsmen in America who play a game they call football. That infamous soul is nicknamed Passionfruit, and he was once a popular star of the sports world in America. He played in the professional football league for a team called the Buffalo Bills. He then starred as an actor and in numerous footballing shows on a device called a television which carries images live into people's homes. He was a hero and a champion but then his reputation took a sinister turn. Passionfruit had a number of affairs during his marriage to Nathalie, and he manipulated her to dress and to wear her hair a certain way. He was known to have a short temper and was jealous of her own relationships even after their divorce. He was put on trial for stabbing her and her friend, Ryan, both of whom were found dead outside her house. The whole world listened to the twists and turns in the story. The trial produced strong evidence of Passionfruit's guilt. People learned that a glove and shoe prints found at the murder scene matched his own. It was a long trial, but to the surprise of many, he was acquitted of the murders. The book he wrote, some years later, effectively contained a confession. The court ordered the book proceeds to go to Ryan's family.'

The Florentine generals

Gradually the boiling blood covered less and less of the souls until just their feet were submerged and, here, we could cross the river safely. About twenty metres ahead of us, I noticed a tributary flowing into the river of blood we were just about to cross, and I made a note to ask Virgil about it as soon as we were alone again.

'As you can see,' the centaur explained, 'the boiling blood gets shallower here, but you can be sure that in the other direction it gets deeper and deeper until it joins the mass murderers again.' Just as he had been commanded, he carried me on his back across the shallowest part of the river and left us to proceed on our journey.

On this side of the riverbank, you could hear the distant sound of water falling far down into the next infernal circle like the throbbing hum of a beehive. A group of three souls came running through the shallow blood scalding their ankles and calling out in unison, 'Stop! Please stop! Your clothes suggest you are from our ill-fated Florence!'

We had met some horrific assassins by now, but Virgil seemed keen to pause one last time before leaving the circle of bloodshed behind us, and I was curious to hear from souls who knew my city well. Virgil advised, 'We should show our respect to these ones. If it wasn't for the boiling blood bubbling under their feet, it should really be you running after them and not the other way round!'

As soon as we stopped, their weeping started up again and when they reached us, the three of them held hands to make a circle. They were like naked, oil-slathered wrestlers walking round the ring, measuring up their opposition before engaging in the fight. Round and round they went with their eyes fixed on me, so that their heads were contorted and faced the opposite direction to their feet.

One of them spoke up. 'It probably pains you to see the blisters and burns on our legs in this vile place, but please don't scorn us or turn away. If we can earn your respect for what we achieved in life, please tell us how you come to be here in your living flesh, absolved from all suffering. The soul I am following may be naked and bald, but he was more important that you may think. His name is Tegghiaio Aldobrandi, mayor of Arezzo and a captain of the Guelph army. He advised the Florentines not to attack the Sienese, but they didn't listen and were defeated in the battle of Montaperti. Fate has us holding hands as in life we could not bridge our divisions, and we spilled pointless blood in power-hungry battles. The thread that binds us together, though, is the land of Tuscany which we strived, in different ways, to defend. It was I, Farinata, who led the Ghibellines to victory at Montaperti. Remember that when my party threatened to raze Florence to the ground, it was I alone who stood out against them, vowing to defend my native city with my own sword. I declared that I was a Florentine first and a Ghibelline second. Following me in the circle of newly made friends is Jacopo Rusticucci, the Florentine nobleman and Guelph warrior.'

If I could have been protected from the boiling blood, I would have leapt down to join them in the river. However, the fear of being burnt to cinders quickly quashed my enthusiasm to hug them all.

With great deference, I said, 'Seeing you now does not make me scornful of you at all. Instead, I feel only sorrow and it will hurt me for some time to come. I am grateful for the opportunity to have met you despite the grave circumstances. I am also from the city of Florence and I have admired your courage and leadership whatever side of the political divide you have fallen on. I am leaving behind the bitterness of sin and am heading for the sweet fruit of salvation promised me by my reliable guide. But to do that, first, I have to plunge down into the depths of this place.'

The corruption of Florence

Farinata then asked, 'As you are living presently in our beloved city, Florence, please tell us if courtesy and courage exist as they once did, as we have heard troubling news from fellow souls.'

I confessed the truth. 'I have no wish to add to your suffering, but Florence weeps uncontrollably. Newcomers in search of a quick buck have generated a culture of greed, vanity and excess in all things.'

The souls nodded sadly as my report confirmed their suspicions. They asked me to tell the world about them and I feel that is the least I can do to earn their respect.

Then they dropped hands to break their circle and fled so fast that their legs might have been wings. They disappeared in the blink of an eye and that was our moment to depart too.

CANTO 16

The Origin of Hell's Rivers

Virgil talks to Dante about the Old Man of Crete, a giant statue hewn from a range of materials whose steady stream of tears flows down into the earth, creating the rivers of Hell. The statue is an allegory for the fall of mankind from innocence and splendour, and its tears represent the accumulation of all the evil and sorrow in the world. The pair then summon a sinister creature called Geryon whose job it is to transport the travellers down from the seventh circle of violent souls to the eighth circle, containing the pits of evil where the fraudulent are punished.

The Old Man of Crete and Hell's rivers

We walked along in silence and, thinking about the rivers which sink so many souls in this frightful place, I begged Virgil to tell me more about them. How they were all so different and where did they end up?

His answer was intriguing. 'Do you remember the little stream we came along after the wood? Well, it pops out on this side of the river too and flows into a waterfall which you have already heard. This stream serves a vital purpose, and I will tell you a story to help you understand. In the middle of the sea, there is a ruined land called Crete whose king, Saturn, reigned a long time ago in a Golden Age of peace and tranquillity. There was a mountain called Ida, once known for its freshwater streams and lush green slopes, but now decayed and abandoned. Saturn's wife, Rhea, who was mother to Jupiter, Neptune and Pluto, chose the mountain as a safe cradle for Jove and a place to hide him from Saturn who wanted to eat his children to stop them from wresting the throne from him. Rhea gave Saturn a stone wrapped in cloth pretending it was Jupiter, and she then fled with her son to the mountain. She had to shout and bash weapons and cymbals to conceal the baby's cries.

'Well, inside that mountain, there is a huge statue of an old man. His back is turned towards Egypt and the East, his face towards Rome and the West, the new world. The composition of the statue reflects the descent of humanity through history. His head is made of finest gold and his arms and chest are made of pure silver. Moving down, he is made of copper until his waist, and, beneath that, he is entirely iron except for his right foot which is made of clay.

He appears to lean more on that clay foot than the other. Every part except the gold, when humanity was in a perfect state, is scarred with a crack from which tears drip down to gather at the statue's feet. Then they forge a torrent flowing down from rock to rock and form the rivers of Hell: Acheron, Styx and Phlegethon. They continue their course through that narrow stream we saw until they come to the dead end that is the pond of Cocytus. You can look forward to learning more when we get there.'

I was struggling to see how it all fitted together and asked, 'If that blood-filled stream originates on Earth, why didn't we see it before reaching the seventh circle?'

'You will have worked out by now that Hell is a round abyss. While we have been turning down to the left, we have not yet completed a whole circle, so don't be surprised if we come across something cutting across our path that we haven't seen before.'

'You haven't mentioned the river Lethe. Where will we see that one?' I asked.

'It's a good question,' he replied, 'but you won't see Lethe in these parts. That river is in the place where souls go to cleanse themselves when they are sorry for their wrongdoings in life to have them washed away.'

Dante's rope

We were now very close to the roaring waterfall and could barely hear each other over the noise. The noise was so powerful that I imagined it must be the world's greatest waterfall. I had a picture in my mind of a wide but gentle river whose journey was spectacularly interrupted to fall in a hundred metre drop down below. We came close to the edge of the rocky cliff where the reddened water tumbled down in a thundering torrent which threatened to deafen our ears.

Virgil examined the fall, and I could see that he was mulling over a plan. He asked me to take off the rope which I was wearing around my waist as a belt. I had thought about using this rope to capture the spotted leopard of self-indulgence which had threatened me at the start of my journey. Now that I had seen the self-indulgent sinners and their torments in the upper part of Hell, I could feel myself growing in moral strength all the time. I no longer needed the rope's protection. I felt sure I could stand firm against whatever evil might lure me in after this, so I untied the knot, rolled the rope into a coil and handed it over to him. Virgil then threw it far out from the edge, and down it went into the deep abyss below.

The ascent of Geryon

I prepared myself for something extraordinary to happen next. Virgil looked intently over the precipice searching for a sign, some sort of response to the ball of rope he had just thrown. Would we see a demon, a centaur or another rabid dog?

Virgil had an amazing way of reading other people's minds and was constantly taking me by surprise. Without even looking in my direction, he said, 'Don't worry, all will be revealed soon enough. The thing I am waiting for and which your imagination is desperately trying to conjure up is about to appear. You will see it right in front of your eyes any moment now.'

His words only increased my feeling of suspense and whatever it was that he had summoned couldn't appear soon enough. I was as excited as I was afraid. The guessing was fun, but I was afraid that I would find the reality too terrifying to bear. I knew from experience that it is often better to say nothing at all than to say something so unbelievable that it seems like an outright lie that makes you appear untrustworthy. But on this occasion, I just couldn't keep it in. Dear reader, I swear by the words of this story that I am telling the truth and it is important that you trust me so that my book may be respected and enjoyed for a long time to come.

Swimming upwards through that thick, black air came a shape which would astound even those who think nothing of the seven wonders of the world. I have seen dolphins gliding through the water, using their tails to leap out of the water as they squeak signals to their companions in their pod. I have seen the bulky weight of hippopotami, known to the Greeks as river horses, forge their way through muddy lakes and rivers grunting and chuffing, and seeking solace in the cooling waters. I have seen a blob-shaped octopus draw up its eight legs into his body before extending them beneath him in a breaststroke action to plough his way to the surface of the sea. But the creature that swam to us now was unlike any of these. In total contrast to the roaring waterfall around us, this sinister creature slunk stealthily towards us in silence.

Geryon; the Arrival in the Circle of Fraud

Geryon is a precursor to the fraudulent sinners Dante and Virgil are about to meet. He is the picture of innocence, but he is hiding his venomous tail and he therefore represents fraud itself. Geryon takes the pair down past the waterfall to the pits of evil in the eighth circle.

Geryon

Virgil gestured a command to the animal to approach the shore near the edge of the stone banks. He then began to talk to me. 'Here is the famous beast with the pointed tail. Like a dragon, he can fly over mountains and, like a Tyrannosaurus Rex, he can break through walls and smash through armies. Look closely at the wretch which pollutes the world!'

The foul picture of fraud came up headfirst, but it left its tail swishing from left to right in the thick air beneath him rather than draw it onto the shore, preferring to keep it hidden. From his face, he looked just like a friendly and respectable man. His skin was clean-shaven and smooth, and his hair was even and short. He had two hairy front paws level with his armpits. The rest of his torso, however, was like a serpent's. His back, chest and sides were painted with stripes and hoops like football shirts, a rainbow of colours intertwined. Neither the Indians nor the Japanese, who are well known for their silks, made fabrics as complex or as rich in colour as this. Not even Arachne designed webs as intricately woven as this and, in case you didn't know, she was the mythical Greek weaving goddess from Lydia who challenged the handicraft goddess, Minerva, to a weaving competition; she was beaten and was turned into a spider!

Imagine a boat recently pulled onto the beach, with its hull in the water and its bow on the sandy shore. Imagine a begging dog, tongue out, whose front paws are up on the table while its hind legs remain grounded on the floor. Imagine a frog submerged in the garden pond, his beady eyes sticking out above the surface as it waits patiently for insects to pass. As the vile beast emerged from the murky depths, it clung to the stone rim of Hell's wall beside our path. His whole tail swished expectantly in the emptiness. Little did I know he had curled up the poisonous fork which armed the tip of his tail like a scorpion.

Virgil said, 'Our path must deviate from the usual direction round to the left as there is nothing routine about fraud. Instead, we need to take a tortuous route towards that evil beast crouching there.'

We made our descent turning to the right, keeping safely to the middle of the path between the river of boiling blood and the animal in the abyss. Virgil then announced that he was going to talk to the beast about lending us his strong shoulders for a ride down to the next circle of Hell. Now, seeing the beast and feeling its danger from the path was one thing, but the idea that we were going to put our trust in him and actually get on his back was quite another. My steps began to slow, and I thought about turning back. But, without Virgil by my side to show me the way back, that didn't seem like an option either.

When I looked up from my anxious deliberations, I saw that Virgil was already straddling the scary beast. 'Come on now,' he said. 'Be strong and brave. We need to confront evil and stay alert in order to protect ourselves and save lives. There is only one way to get down below and this is it. You get on in front and I'll sit behind you so that the poisonous sting in the tail can't reach you.'

I felt like someone struggling to breathe after an allergic reaction or frozen so stiff by the wintry air that their lips, and the tips of their fingers turn blue. My whole body shivered at the thought of being surrounded by darkness, but shame at my cowardice spurred me on with false courage as I didn't want to disappoint my worthy and noble guide. I got myself seated, albeit shakily, on those frightful shoulders and I wanted to speak to Virgil, but I couldn't find my voice to say, 'Please put your arms around me'.

My perceptive guide, who anticipated my thoughts and feelings, and who had helped me before when I struggled with moments of doubt, wrapped his arms around me and supported me as soon as I got on. Then he commanded the beast, 'Geryon, move yourself now. Go down in wide circles so that the ride is gradual and controlled. Think about the new weight you are carrying.'

Like the little boat I described earlier, which inches back off its moorings from the beach into the water, the beast launched himself off from the bank. When he felt completely free of the rocky edge, he turned himself around and, stretching out his tail as if it was a rudder, he moved like an eel pushing the dense air away and pulling himself through its fetid vapours.

I felt no less fear than did Phaeton, the son of Helios the sun god, when he lost his reins. Phaeton had persuaded his father to let him drive his chariot of Sun for the day. However, Phaeton was too weak to hold the horses who bolted close to the earth, almost setting it on fire. Jupiter saved Earth by striking Phaeton with a thunderbolt and making him fall into the river Po. You will always be able to see the tracks where Phaeton's chariot scorched the sky when you look at the multitude of stars making the Milky Way.

Nor was my fear any less than that of the unfortunate Icarus, son of Daedulus, when he flew too close to the sun. He felt himself losing his feathers as the wax that was meant to hold them melted. His father shouted to him, "You are going the wrong way!" He promptly landed up in the Aegean Sea.

I was far more afraid than either of them when I realised that I was in the middle of a black hole and my eyes could not penetrate the terrible darkness beyond the beast's back – where I had no desire to be.

On the beast went, slowly round and round, down and down, but I had no sense of our movement except for the draft on my face coming up from below. And then I could hear the gorge at the base of the waterfall booming loudly to our right-hand side. When I peered over to take a look, the fear of alighting from the beast's back was worse than staying on! I could see leaping flames and wailing voices. At that moment, I started shaking all over and gripped my steed harder with my knees.

Finally, I saw what I hadn't been able to see previously. We were swooping and gliding down and round through more and more tormented souls who were pressing in on us from all sides. As we completed our descent, Geryon became like a reluctant dog that doesn't want to go out in the rain. When his owner calls him brightly, he just droops his ears, lowers his head and takes a few sulky steps towards his owner before crouching down in disdainful protest. This was how Geryon landed. Perhaps he was brooding because he had been forced by a higher command to carry us travellers or perhaps, as the face of fraud, he had hoped to deceive his riders but missed his opportunity. Geryon set us down at the foot of the rock face and, having relieved himself of his burden, sprung away like a missile fired from a catapult.

Liars and Cheats

Concealed in Flames

The eighth circle of Hell contains ten circular ditches nicknamed "Evil Pits" for those who have committed fraud. They are like the moats you'd find around medieval castles and are crossed by bridges. The ditches are arranged in diminishing concentric rings with the icy lake of Cocytus at the centre. The landscape is increasingly rocky and iron-grey as the atmosphere gets less recognisably human on the approach to Hell's centre. The first ditch contains liars and cheats. Through their deceptive words and actions, they have lost all integrity and, as punishment, they are hidden inside flames. As communication was the tool of deception, their tongues are rendered useless, and they can only speak through the flame.

Description of "Evil Pits"

There is a place in Hell called "Evil Pits". It is full of iron-grey slate just like the cliffs surrounding it. Right in the middle of this evil space lies a pond which is fairly wide and deep. I am going to try and explain how it is laid out.

The eighth circle of Hell sits between the pond and the foot of the craggy high cliff which we had just descended on Geryon's back. The circle is separated into ten valleys or ditches, each containing a different sort of fraudulent sinner. They have all deceived other people one way or another and they are ranked in order of the gravity of their sin as determined by Minos.

Imagine a moat surrounding a castle to protect it from the enemy. Normally, you will see drawbridges which allow people to cross the moat, but they can also be lifted to shut the enemy out. Now imagine not just a single moat but a series of concentric moats surrounding the castle, each with its own drawbridge that takes you to the next moat. In the same way, these valleys had rocky bridges intersecting them from the cliff at the outer edge, right the way to the central pond.

Geryon shook us off his burdened back and here we were, in this strange and eerie place. Virgil assumed his usual direction, turning to the left and I followed closely in his wake.

Liars and cheats

On the right-hand side, I saw quite a different scene unfold. In this first ditch, thousands of flames were gleaming and flickering like city lights at night seen from a mountain top. All along the base of the ditch you could see brilliant yellow flames, but it was impossible to see through them. I thought of the prophet Elijah who was whisked away in his chariot to Heaven. His companion Elisha watched him from the ground, but he couldn't see either the prophet or the magnificent horses as they were wrapped in a flame which got smaller and smaller the higher it went, wafting in the sky like a wisp of cloud.

I was standing on the bridge on the tips of my toes and would have toppled over the edge if I hadn't been gripping a rock. Virgil saw my keen interest and explained, 'I think you may have guessed as much, but inside each of those flames there is a sinner who has effectively enclosed himself within his torment.'

Elizabeth Taylor

'I did think the souls must be contained within those flames but, try as I might to see through them from up here, I couldn't be sure. Now you've confirmed it, I know you are right. Can you tell me who that flame is that seems to quiver more than most?'

Virgil told me, 'That is the soul of a woman who will become a famous actress many years from now. She has an extraordinary story, and you might even find it entertaining if you ask her to tell you about herself. In tune with the circle of Hell she finds herself in, she was married eight times and she even married one of her husbands twice! She is here because she cheated on most of her husbands and thought nothing of having affairs with dozens of rich and famous men.'

'Well, if these sparks speak, I will gladly listen!' I was eager to learn the colourful story that oozed vice.

Virgil called on the flame to stop for a moment and talk to us and I asked her to reveal her name. Her flame began to quiver as if blown about by the wind and then, as the tip flicked up and down like a talking tongue, a voice forced its way out and said, 'I am Elizabeth Taylor, but people may also remember me as Cleopatra. I found happiness and destruction in love in equal measure. I was unable to manage long term relationships because I kept wanting something new, or, in the case of one of my marriages, I was left bereft and widowed by a tragically premature death. For me, it was not the having but the getting. I suffered plenty of heartache, but I also know I caused a lot of heartache to others. At my worst, I cheated on one husband by breaking up the marriage of a dear friend. I loved fame and fortune, but the wheel of love kept spinning. My deceptions have landed me here. I am a lost and grieving soul with nothing to clothe me but a fiery flame. Even my famous diamond jewellery has lost all value in this flaming Hell.'

I wanted to hear more. 'Why don't you tell me about how you arrived here after the fame you enjoyed in life?'

'One fine day – I was feeling pretty sickly by then – a devil grabbed me by the hair and took me out of the world. He delivered me to Minos whose tail of judgement coiled itself eight times round that rump and, laying his teeth into his tail in a rage, he said: "This one must be thrown amongst the thieving flames for having thieved so many lovers from their wives!'

The flame became still and steady again when she stopped speaking, and we let her go on her way. I was moved by this story of love, but my heart hardened when I heard how she had chosen to lie behind the backs of so many husbands. You can be unfortunate in love, and I have seen many examples of that in arranged or rushed marriages, but infidelity of this order represents a series of hurtful choices and I understood why her prison was made of fire.

Virgil showed me the flame of Catherine the Great who was to become a Russian Empress but who cheated on her husband with a string of men, including, as time went by, some many years younger than herself. He told me that she was generous to her lovers and gave them jewellery, land and titles, but this generosity did not wash away her deceit and she had to pay a price far higher than the value of her earthly gifts in this eternal hellfire.

Horatio Nelson

A little further on, I noticed a strangely lopsided flame. Virgil explained that the soul had lost his arm in life and his eternal flame hugged the shape of his body revealing a kink. I mustered up some courage to talk to the flame directly. 'One-armed soul, tell me who you are and what brings you to this bonfire of vanities?'

The flame sputtered and spat and finally a voice came out. 'I am in burning pain, but I would like to share my story with you. Horatio Nelson is my name. If you lived in the future, you would hail me for stemming Napoleon's tide of supremacy which was to destroy your blessed Holy Roman Empire. I trumped the French emperor's sea powers and thwarted his attempt to conquer England. I was a hero for the British when I led the navy to victory in the Battle of Trafalgar, but my honours are tainted by my vice. I deceived my loyal wife, Frances, and repaid her faithfulness with infidelity. Not only did I deceive her, but I took my lover, Emma Hamilton, away from the marital breast of one of my closest friends and deceived him too. I cannot regret the happiness I found in Emma and in our wonderful daughter, Horatia, whose paternity was my final lie.'

I told him, 'I am sure the greatness of your achievements will live for ever in the world, but your medals are worthless here, destroyed by the flame that will never lie.'

I have lived much of my life in the hope that Italy could once again be governed by a cohesive and respected Roman Empire so that intercity feuds and fights could be set aside for good. I longed for stability in government and a society bound by well-enforced laws. I was deeply troubled by the news that a French enemy was to destroy the magnificent Roman Empire, and that further fighting between peoples and nations was destined to ensue down the ages.

Ulysses' Last Voyage; the Journey to the Southern Hemisphere

Dante and Virgil meet some more liars and cheats before being treated to the truth about Ulysses' last voyage. We see that human capacity for thinking and doing great things are only truly great if they sit within moral bounds. If we use our intelligence to pervert moral norms, then we are perverting God's gifts and we will be judged for that after death.

Ulysses and his men reach the other side of the world to see Mount Purgatory in the distance, believed in medieval times to be the only land in the Southern Hemisphere. Heroic Ulysses fails because to succeed in such an unprecedented challenge requires help from divine grace, a privilege which is unavailable to him as he lived before Christ's time. His failure reflects the inadequacy of humanity in the absence of God. These ancients achieved greatness but only in so far as human reason allowed. Ulysses' journey is a tragedy and contrasts with Dante's journey which will have a happy resolution. Dante is supported by divine grace and will ultimately find happiness in salvation.

Diego Maradona nicknamed "The Golden Boy"

I was not left to my thoughts for long as I was distracted by a strange roar. The sound was coming out of the tip of a new-looking flame close by. There was no outlet, no escape for these prisoners' voices, so the trapped words bubbled up in a strange language until they found their way out at the tip.

The tip of this flame could be seen quivering with vibrations sent up by the tongue and the vocal cords, and we heard, 'Remind those people, lucky enough to enjoy the sun and the rain on the green fields, about my story! They called it the "Hand of God" but that was the lucky strike. The second shot was called: "Goal of the century". I knew I was a genius and a hero for the world. But to keep my reputation alive, I needed to be greater. That hand of God let me down in the end and has banished me to this dumb misery.'

When he had finished speaking, the weeping flame departed, jolting and jerking its pointed tip. Virgil explained that this soul had made his name in a game people will come to call football and that the sport was a global phenomenon. 'He was caught cheating at the very sport he loved and in which he had excelled. He filled his body with illegal substances to enhance his performance on (and off) the pitch and was disgraced, although his many supporters and even his team-mates continued to idolise him.'

As Virgil led the way again, I considered how easy it is for heroes to fall and realised how difficult it is to reconcile greatness with humanity. Is mankind too weak to ride the wave of greatness. Is that a state only truly worthy of a superior being untouched by our fallibility?

Ulysses and Diomedes

Virgil called back to me, 'You see the flame ahead with two tips? Suffering inside together are Ulysses and Diomedes. They are combined in punishment as they were combined in combat. In that burning flame, they grieve over the lie that the Trojan horse was a gift to Athena, the goddess of war, pretending that the Greeks had abandoned the war effort and were ceding victory to the Trojans. You will remember that this was far from the truth. Out came the Greek soldiers hidden in the wooden horse to pillage Troy, leaving it in ashes. They also dared to steal the statue of Pallas whose presence was believed to protect the city. Now these two must suffer for the suffering they caused.'

I begged Virgil, 'When the horned flame reaches us, please, please stop it so that I can hear more. I know that you know the story I want to hear.'

Ulysses describes his last voyage

When Virgil felt it was the right moment to stop the flame, I heard him say, 'You two in the one flame, if the words I crafted about you in my poem make me even a little deserving of your time, please indulge me for a moment. Now that there is no scope for lies, please tell us the truth about how you were lost and went to die.'

The taller peak of the ancient flame wobbled from side to side and the tip tensed in an effort to push the words out. At last, a voice emerged. 'For twelve months, I had stayed with the sorceress Circe on her island. When I finally departed, it wasn't into the arms of my elderly father or my abandoned wife, Penelope, or my beloved son. Sadly not. No sense of duty or love could quench my desire to explore and know the world, to understand all human vice and all human virtue. I set sail on the open sea in just one boat with a small crew who had stood by me all this time. I went from shore to shore until I sighted Spain, Morocco, Sardinia and the other lands that bathe in the Mediterranean Sea. My companions and I were old and arthritic when we reached the Strait of

Gibraltar, where Hercules set out his pillars to mark the limits of the world beyond which no man should go. We had Spain to our right and Morocco to our left. "Brothers," I said, "for all those hundreds and thousands of dangers you have faced and overcome to get to this point, we only have a short time left of our lives and we shouldn't deny ourselves the experience of following the sun further round the world to the place where no man has been. Remember who you are. You were born not as beasts but as humans with the gift of intellect, and your destiny is to follow virtue and knowledge."

'My short oration roused such eagerness in my companions to set off on our mission that I could barely hold them back. We set our course for the west and propelled our oars like wings for the foolish flight, pulling harder to starboard in order to bear to our left. We could see the stars blazing brightly at the start of night in the Antarctic sky while the Arctic stars were so low that they were barely visible above the horizon. Five monthly moons had passed since we set off on our voyage to the deep when the outline of a mountain emerged in the distance. I was sure it was the highest I had ever seen. We were overjoyed but sadly not for long. Our spirits were dashed as a whirlwind whipped itself up from the shores of the approaching land, and it struck our boat on the bow. It spun us round three times in a vortex of water and, the fourth time, it lifted the stern clean out of the water and plunged the bow down below until the sea closed over our heads just as God had intended.'

The voice fizzled out although its flame kept blazing as it proceeded on its new journey, eternally confined within the dreary grey walls of the ditch. I was moved by Ulysses' story and reflecting back on it now makes me feel sad all over again. It also makes me conscious of the need to use my knowledge carefully so that it doesn't lead me to deceive people or want more than is my due. If I have been blessed with the gifts of knowledge and understanding, I should not abuse them.

Thieves

Metamorphosis between Snakes and Human Forms

Here are the thieves who have their hands bound behind their backs: the very hands which took from other people. They have no control over their physical form as some metamorphose into snakes and back again. They are now destined to be consumed by evil.

The pit of thieves

We had reached the point where the narrow path crosses to the second bank and forms an abutment for another bridge. The depths of the next ditch were so gloomy that the only place to stand and see everything was the centre of the bridge where the arch was at its highest.

We climbed to that point and peered into the darkness below. Writhing in the pit beneath us was an entangled mass of snakes of all different shapes and sizes. Picturing it now makes my blood curdle. Rattlesnakes, vipers, mambas, adders and cobras seethed and coiled in some sort of cruel and abandoned zoo. However, these snakes did not deserve any pity; they hissed hatred and their venomous fangs were poised to poison. We saw terrified, naked souls darting about through this cold-blooded and threatening throng, desperately searching for a safe place to hide. There was clearly no hope of healing from those ferocious fangs.

The souls' hands were bound behind them and, when I looked closely, I was surprised to see that they weren't tied with rope but with more snakes whose heads and tails pushed through their legs coiling themselves in knots about their private parts.

A metamorphosis

At the outer edge of the ditch near where we stood, we watched a pair of shivering souls seeking shelter. They were talking animatedly to each other and I could see them sometimes nodding, sometimes shaking their heads. I guessed they were devising a plan of escape. However, escape certainly didn't look like an option in this place and, as if proof was needed, their prison walls were about to close in on them. A pair of closely intertwined cobras, who had been lying quite still near their feet, suddenly leapt up and coiled themselves around one neck each, paralysing them with a single bite.

Quicker than you or I could call "watch out!", the souls burst into flames and fell to the ground in a pile of ash. No sooner had the ash settled on the dusty floor, than the pieces picked themselves up and resumed their human form.

Have you heard the mythical stories of the majestic phoenix? It is said that the phoenix dies and is reborn out of the flames five hundred years later. The phoenix does not live off grass and grain like other birds; it is nourished with drops of incense and cardamom. When it dies, it makes itself a nest of myrrh, honeysuckle and spices, and falls into a deep sleep for hundreds of years until it is time to rise again. Seeing the transformation in these souls reminded me of the phoenix's rebirth and made me think that perhaps truth could be born out of myth.

You have probably seen someone have an epileptic fit or perhaps just a faint brought on by an allergic reaction, or a rush of blood or oxygen away from the brain. It is as if they are dragged down to the earth by some terrible and otherworldly force and then, when they come round again, they get up looking around them all dazed and confused.

These sorry souls looked just like that as they staggered about in their renewed human forms, trying to find their feet. Their heads drooped low in sad resignation at finding themselves in the same wretched pit as before. All powerful God, the blows of divine justice come down hard on those who have angered you!

Bonnie and Clyde

Virgil called out to the unsteady souls and asked them who they were. The woman replied, 'I am Bonnie, and I am stuck in this Hell with Clyde. We were well known across a large country which will be new to you, called America. It is a respected power in the western world enjoying freedom and democracy and we loved it well.'

At this point, I became intrigued and took up the interrogation. 'If you loved your country so well, then what sin has banished you to this place? What can you have done which is worse than anger and violence?'

'Love for your country and for your family isn't always enough to keep you from starving. America was stuck in a deep depression and jobs and money were hard to come by. It was particularly bad in the poor south where I lived with my folks. I thought I might make a career as a singer or an actress, as I have always loved the shows and enjoyed being centre stage in the school pageants. I did find fame, but it wasn't a clean route in, and it wasn't the sort I had first planned for. I married young to a man whose selfish pranks and excessive drinking landed him behind bars, so I knew what crime was all about. When I met my friend here, Clyde, I discovered a new excitement in earning money from robberies. It was easier to raid shops and banks than to find a job earning a decent living. Unfortunately for the victims, there were murders along the way, but we had to eliminate a number of street authorities to get our booty. Now here we are, tossed by Minos into the evil of the eighth circle.'

I was intrigued to know how theft could be judged to be worse than murder. I encouraged her to tell me more.

'We had to plan our attacks carefully, although we were often disorganised and came away with paltry sums compared with the risks we were running. Murder is a sin of violence and clearly hurts other people, but theft harms more than the person. It harms their possessions and their livelihoods too because they are taken away. The economic impact of theft, however big or small, is judged to be a greater affront to society.'

'And how did you become famous with your evil ways?' I asked.

'Infamous really. Our tally of murders reached the unlucky number thirteen. We also got away with breaking friends out of jail, and robbing shops and banks all over the mid-south. We posted pictures of ourselves smoking cigars and messing with stolen vehicles and we created an image that we were above the law which made the authorities mad to catch us. You know, it would have been a lonely existence without Clyde and our gang, and I wouldn't have done it without him. Clyde played his saxophone, which is a sort of modern-day trumpet, and, with his accompaniment, I sang our favourite songs. That saxophone just kept on tooting until the toots became gun shots which peppered our heads. It was Clyde's saxophone that sounded on that judgement day.'

Bonnie fell silent at this moment but then she took up her story again one last time. 'I would like you to share my poem with the world if you make it back there from this cruel place. I called it "The end of the line" because I thought life would end in death. Look how wrong I was! Little did I think that the consequences of my actions would cause me such terrible suffering after death. Here I am, robbed of my identity, an identity which I had proudly crafted to set me apart from the rest.'

She then gave me these words which were her own prophesy:

> *"They don't think they're too smart or desperate,*
> *They know the law always wins;*
> *They've been shot at before,*
> *But they do not ignore*
> *That death is the wages of sin.*
>
> *Someday they'll go down together;*
> *And they'll bury them side by side,*
> *To a few it'll be grief –*
> *To the law a relief –*
> *But it's death for Bonnie and Clyde.'*

I thought about how many people think life ends with death and that their choices, good or bad, have no further meaning after they have died. I believed that good people who live their lives well will find happiness forever and, right now, I was learning that those who make bad choices which harm other people in their life, pay for those choices in eternal torment.

Metamorphosis

Thieving Forms

Dante and Virgil meet the arch thief who used his mastery of disguise to steal jewellery, works of art and other valuable items. The thieves must endure ever-changing bodies and be forever associated with snakes reflecting their slippery, stealthy natures.

Arsène Lupin

Our eyes settled on another thieving soul who was remarkable because, unlike the other souls who were naked, he was wearing a black top hat and a long black cloak. He also had a round glass over one eye. He was standing tall and seemed to float over the bodies of the snakes which writhed in the bottom of the pit.

Virgil raised his voice so that the soul could hear and said, 'I have overheard souls discussing that top-hatted thief. His reputation and the stories of his evil tricks are notorious in all of Hell. He is called Arsène Lupin and is known as "the gentleman thief" although his wicked ruses are hardly suited to such a title.'

When the soul realised that we were talking about him, he became irritated that his identity had been found out, and Virgil was prompted to provoke him. 'If you insist on wearing your trickster's outfit, you cannot expect to go unrecognised. You are as stealthy as the snakes which slither and slide between your toes.'

Lupin turned a deep red and exploded in rage, 'The pain I feel at being recognised in this wretched place is worse than the pain of death. I have been sent to this ditch because I stole the most precious jewels known to man. Still, no one was clever enough to catch me, as I kept changing my disguise. Even God is having trouble pinning me down in Hell as I slip into my many characters. I am at once the jester, the law enforcer, the prisoner, the rich traveller and the retired general. Catch me if you can!" And with that, he stuck up two fingers on both hands, crying: "This is for you, God!'

I had not seen such an insolent soul in all the circles of this bitter Hell, and from that moment on, I sided with the snakes in my desire to see his wicked arrogance punished. I was actually pleased to see one of the snakes coil itself around Lupin's neck as if to say, "You will be silenced!" Another snake wrapped itself around his arms and bound him tight between the legs so that he couldn't move an inch. As soon as the venomous fang approached his neck, the conspicuous cloak and handsome hat went up in flames and the newly naked soul scarpered across the snake pit.

The centaur Cacus

My wonder didn't cease when I saw an angry centaur trot by in pursuit of the sinful soul. 'Right, where is he, that rebel Lupin?' The centaur's back was covered in squirming snakes which hung down on either flank. Clinging to his shoulders, behind the nape of his human neck, there was a green and black dragon with outstretched wings, breathing fire on anyone who crossed his path.

Virgil explained, 'That is Cacus, the son of Vulcan, god of fire. Cacus lived in a rocky cave in a remote mountain called Mount Aventine and, according to the stories, he made many lakes of blood out of his killing sprees. He isn't with his brother centaurs who guard the violent souls submerged in the river Phlegethon, but he is condemned here due to his cunning theft of the oxen which he hid in his cave. His wicked deeds came to an end when Hercules clubbed him to death with a hundred blows, although his life gave out after just ten.'

Lupin's disguises and a second metamorphosis

The centaur galloped past while my guide was speaking and, at the same time, three souls appeared below us. Neither of us had noticed them until our conversation was interrupted by their shouting, 'What are you doing here?'

Virgil explained that each of these souls was in fact Lupin in disguise. He was being punished several times over, each of his many personas receiving the same torment. As he had stolen and assumed a different identity each time, now he was suffering the pain of transformation for each one of those identities, as you will see. Virgil challenged me, 'The clue is in the name, see if you can keep a track of who is who!'

Upon my word, dear reader, if it takes you a while to believe what I am about to tell you that wouldn't surprise me. I saw it with my eyes and could scarcely believe it myself.

One of the souls called out, 'Where has Sernine got to?' I fixed my gaze on the speaking soul and saw a lizard, with six feet no less, spring up in front of the sinner and cling on with its claws. The central claws clasped the soul's stomach while the front claws clasped the arms. It then revealed its fangs, lancing one cheek and then the other. The creature's hind claws were stretched out across the soul's thighs and its tail threaded through his legs between his butt cheeks.

Not even ivy clings to a tree as tightly as this animal entwined itself limb around limb. Then, just like hot wax, they melted into each other and their colours merged, like paints mixing, into a new combination.

The other two souls stood nearby, their mouths gaping. 'Oh, great goodness, Perenna, look how you've changed! You are no longer one or even two.'

The two heads had become one and, although each face had gone, they were now fused together in some weird technological wonder. The upper limbs became two new arms, and the legs, stomach and chest became an altogether new, horrid amalgamation of the sort never seen before. You could recognise nothing of what they were. The perverse picture depicted both and neither. Then, on its newly found feet, it dragged itself away.

Third metamorphosis

Like a gecko darting in a flash from shrub to shrub in the midday sun, a fearsome and fiery snake, black as black pepper, came scampering out from nowhere, intent on capturing the bellies of the two remaining souls. It launched itself at one of them, clamped its jaws down hard, but fell instantly to the ground in a heap. The poisoned soul stood dazed, unable to speak, unable to move. Then, as if stunned by sleep or sickness, he stretched open his mouth in a yawn.

He looked at the snake and the snake looked at him. Trails of smoke poured out from both the victim's wound and the attacker's mouth, and soon the floating trails blended together as one.

You may have read stories of changing monsters in the books of Lucan or Ovid but those are nothing to this. The ancient poets told stories of people turning into monsters or matter, and you will have read stories about people having avatars, but I doubt you will have ever heard of two forms exchanging their bodily beings. Just wait till you hear what happened next.

With exact symmetry, the snake's tail split in two like a fork, and the injured soul's feet now became one followed by its legs and thighs until not even a chink of light pierced the freshly moulded flesh.

The forked tail took on the features of human legs and the scaled skin became soft and smooth while the soul's skin became rough and scaly. I saw the soul's arms shrink at the armpits just as the beast's feet were sprouting into legs. Then the snake's central claws clasped each other and became a human penis, and from the miserable soul's testicles burst forth two feet.

The smoke swirled and shrouded the scene so that it was increasingly difficult to tell which was which or who was who. One became hairy and the other hairless; one stood up and the other fell to the ground. Each kept their eyes intently focused on the other as the horrific transformation was so painfully fascinating for each of them to witness.

The snake's nostrils sucked themselves into the face and the excess flesh found its way out through the smooth cheeks as ears, then nose, then human lips. The soul's nose became a snout, and he drew in his ears like a snail draws in his tentacles. The tongue, which was once used for speaking, now split in two, and in the other, the forked tongue filled out. Then the smoke cleared. The newly formed monster fled hissing through the valley and the newly formed human chased after him spitting speech.

The metamorphosed man turned his new shoulders to the third soul who stood gawping and said, 'I want to see Nespi scamper round the track on all fours like I did.'

I saw so many changes and permutations in that second ditch that I am sorry if my retelling doesn't do it justice. Although my eyes were confused and my mind baffled, the turmoil around those fleeing sinners failed to disguise a moment of truth in my mind. Playing all these changes back in my mind, and remembering Virgil's clue about the names, I realised that Arsène Lupin used the letters of his name to play a game with the authorities and the world, tricking and deceiving them to carry out his thefts. Here were his characters all around us. Arsène Lupin, Sernine, Perenna and Nespi were the same person. One disguised as many. Many disguised as one.

Kidnappers

Sliced by Demons

As Dante and Virgil journey into the third ditch, they meet the souls of kidnappers. These sinners are repeatedly sliced with a sword by a demon, a reflection of how they ripped apart families by robbing them of their children, often killing the abducted child in the process. The punishment is repeated over and over again just as the victims' families are often forced to live without closure. They are left with the desperate and probably futile hope that they may see their child again.

The kidnappers

Virgil and I pressed on along the rocky ravine until we reached the next bridge over the ditch where sinners who have kidnapped or abducted children receive their just deserts.

Who could possibly, even with the benefit of vivid adjectives and clever similes, describe the blood and the wounds I now saw before me? No storyteller could, with the limitations of human sight and mind, capture the scenes I witnessed and then adequately convey them.

If all the dead and wounded from all the wars and battles ever fought were brought together in one spot to reveal their torn, bloody and mangled limbs, the scene wouldn't do anything like justice to the one I now saw before me in the hideous third ditch.

I saw a soul whose front side gaped open like an oversized unbuttoned jacket. His body was ripped apart from the neck right to the hole where he farts, and his insides hung down between his legs. You could see his heart, liver and lungs dangling out as well as the foul intestines which convert suppers to shit.

While I gawped at him in utter horror, he stared back at me and proceeded to rip open his own breast even further with his bare hands saying, 'Look how I can split myself apart! All of us you see here are kidnappers. We abducted children from their families, tearing them apart from their loved ones and breaking family bonds. For that we are ripped apart in death. There is a demon on guard who cruelly and repeatedly slices us apart with his sword every time we circle round in front of him on this dismal track. As we complete the full circle our wounds are more or less healed only to be split open again by that cleaving sword. But who are you loiterers, inspecting us from the bridge? Perhaps you have got lost on the way to your allocated punishment?'

Virgil replied for us. 'The man I accompany is neither dead, nor a sinner. He is still alive in his flesh and, although I am dead myself, it is my duty to show him all of Hell by leading him down and round this spiralling staircase of sin. You have heard my words. You had better believe them.'

Suddenly the eyes of hundreds of souls were on us as they stopped in their tracks to look at me in amazement, forgetting their suffering just for a moment.

The Beaumont children's kidnapper

Virgil asked the speaking soul who was torn in two to tell us the nature of his sin and how his punishment was so extensive.

'It happened one afternoon when I myself took to loitering along the beach in a sunny southern country known as Australia. Like all the souls here, we suffer a mental sickness which prompts us to fill a need. What I needed that day was to steal away a child. I had stationed myself near the bus stop for the beach, waiting for the right moment. A bus, much like the carts you will know from your own time, could carry tens of people from one destination to another. When a little boy and a girl were led off the bus by their older nine-year-old sister, I knew this was my chance.

'The children were making their way to the beach for an outing by themselves. Life was typically free-range in Australia in the 1960s. I distracted the youngest child by pretending there was a kitten stuck under a vehicle parked just by the bus stop. That vehicle was mine. As the children crouched down to look, I managed to pick up the oldest girl and stuffed her onto the back seat. The younger two put up less of a fight, as they instinctively wanted to stay with their older sister. Then they were mine.

'I got away with two further child abductions after that. I scooped two from the Adelaide Oval and another two near their school where I worked as a carpenter. The world heard these stories and wept with the families but there was not enough evidence to convict me. It is too late now to mend all those broken hearts. Death comes to us all, but my pain of death is eternal. Under the slicing sword, this heart will never mend. You can tell the world what you have seen as they will be desperate for answers to their questions.'

He said these words mid-stride and then proceeded on his way.

John Paul Getty III's kidnapper

Another soul who had a hole in his throat, his nose cut clean off and only one ear, stopped with the others to gaze at me in amazement. Widening his bloodied throat to talk, he said, 'I took the boy for money. The Getty family had more wealth than they knew what to do with. It was an empire built off natural resources. I reckoned they could part with a bit of money to satisfy my needs. But the grandfather was greedy, and he refused my ransom, so I cut off the boy's ear and sent it to him in the post to make him see I meant business. The problem was that the boy was a rebel and had repeatedly joked about faking a kidnap in order to wheedle money out of his stingy grandfather, so nobody believed it when it actually happened. The boy had cried wolf too often. I got the money, eventually, and John Paul Senior has been cast into the fourth circle above, amongst the money grubbers. As for me, well, for that ear which I sliced, I have had an ear and my nose and throat sliced and resliced, over and over again.'

Charles Lindbergh Junior's kidnapper

I saw a soul who had both hands cut off, punching the thick black air with his bleeding stumps and spraying blood all over his face. If that wasn't abhorrent enough, I am not sure I can describe the next thing I saw without a witness to back me up. However, I know I am telling the truth and that gives me the courage to share it with you. I promise I saw, and I can still see it in my mind's eye now, a body walking along without a head. The soul was holding his severed head by the hair, swinging it in his hand like a lantern.

The loose head spotted us and said, 'Show me some mercy!' The soul had made a lamp for itself of his own head. The two body parts belonged together as one, but now they were cruelly divided.

When he reached the foot of the bridge where we were standing, he lifted his arm up high to bring his head closer to us so we could clearly hear his words. 'Look closely at my terrible suffering, you who live and breathe and visit the dead. I am Bruno Hauptmann who took the two-month-old baby from the Lindbergh family home for ransom. Charles Lindbergh was a wealthy man and, if you remind the world about me, they will come to know that he made his name for piloting the first transatlantic flight travelling from New York City to Paris without stopping.

'One night, I climbed hastily up my rickety ladder to the second floor and squeezed in through the window. I managed to take the sleeping baby but there was not enough light to see what I was doing and, as I was descending that ladder backwards, a rung broke midway down. I slipped and dropped the baby to the ground, and he was killed instantly. I needed to keep the death a secret in order to earn the ransom money. The authorities had the public and even the criminal underworld try to catch me, but I eventually got the money and could move up out of life as a carpenter. The lack of light which caused me to bungle the kidnapping has come back to bite me now though. God has made a lantern out of my head and, for pulling that family apart, I am torn in two. They electrocuted me to death in the chair and, witness the irony, I am now doomed to carry my brain, cut off from its connections until no spark is left.'

CANTO 23

Paedophiles

Submerged in Human Excrement

In the fourth ditch of Evil Pits, we meet paedophiles who are plunged in human excrement. In life they preyed on innocence to satisfy their warped and depraved sexual desires. It is a phenomenon which has existed since Greek and Roman times, but it is shocking to the modern world and we are rightly keen to see perpetrators justly punished.

Emperor Tiberius

I felt weakened by the stories of so much evil and the sight of so much suffering. Virgil could see I was flagging, and he quickly put both arms round me and lifted me to his chest. He carried me back along the rocky path which led to the next bridge, marking the pathway from the third to the fourth ditch. He did not put me down until we were safely at the top of the bridge. Once we were there, he unburdened himself gently as the rock was jagged and steep, really only safe for hardy mountain goats.

We could hear souls whimpering in the ditch below us, puffing and snuffling like pigs through their mouths and noses, and slapping themselves with the palms of their hands. The banks were caked with mould from the fetid air which made your eyes water and your nose wrinkle in disgust.

Peering down through the stinking darkness from the highest point of the bridge, I could see souls marinading in manure which looked very much like piles of human shit. While I was searching for a soul I might recognise in the depths, I saw one with his head covered in so much filth that you couldn't tell whether he had a full head of hair or whether he was bald, whether his hair was blond or black. This one lamented, 'Why are you so intent on looking at me rather than the other filthy wretches?'

As he wriggled about, some of the muck slipped off his head. I noticed a liver spot on his forehead, and I recognised the short curly fringe, the signature of the Roman emperors. 'You are Emperor Tiberius, are you not? You can't deny your identity here! You were only marginally less ugly in life by all accounts. I know of your evil deeds but, tell me, what specific sin has landed you in this horrible cesspit?'

Tiberius lifted his hands in despair and started striking his head with a fist. 'I will answer your question but don't let people forget the success of my military campaigns in Europe for the Roman Empire. Emperor Augustus had no other choice than me to take his place on the imperial throne. I was not well suited to the role and, leaving my senators to run state affairs, I took refuge on the pretty island of Capri which people came to call, rather deprecatingly, the "old goat's garden". There I indulged in lavish parties and tied up the genitals of my guests to prevent them from urinating out the flagons of wine I made them consume. I took advantage of young boys to satisfy my sexual cravings. I enjoyed taking a bath in the garden and had my "little fish" nibble and satisfy my sex under water. A sense of power over my child pawns made up for my feelings of failure as a leader. Still, nothing prepared me for the eternal stinking slurry that I am condemned to roll in now.'

Jimmy Savile

We left him to sink back in the shit and Virgil said, 'Now look a bit further on in front of us and you will see the face of a foul, dishevelled soul who is scratching himself with his shit filled fingernails, and who bobs up and down between squatting and standing. He is holding what will become known in the future as a cigar and he wears great chunky chains around his neck and wrists. He will be known to the world as Jimmy Savile. His sin is all the more gruesome as he was a hero in some children's eyes. Young boys and girls knew they could write a letter to Jimmy Savile telling him what they wanted to do or see in their wildest dreams, and, if they were lucky, he would make their dreams come true. He enabled children to meet famous singers and artists; they could visit famous landmarks or skydive from a flying vehicle which, as you have heard already, they now call a plane. He seemed to do many good things for society, running marathons and raising large sums of money for charities. However, for each building block he constructed to strengthen society, he sent other blocks tumbling down. In the public eye, he appeared to be making society a better place but behind closed doors he was destroying the fabric of that very society.'

I was curious to know how so much apparent good could be undone and I asked, 'What terrible things did he do to break society? How and why?'

'That man preyed on defenceless and vulnerable children. He found them in hospitals, in care homes and in schools which he visited on the pretext of bringing brightness into children's lives. He abused, raped or molested hundreds of children in care because he was depraved, and he knew these children would be the least likely to resist and the least likely to be listened to. His fame made him untouchable. He didn't want a relationship where he'd be required to give something back. With the children, he just took what he wanted, without consent and with impunity. Every child he abused or molested was a broken block for society.'

RC-F2

I felt nothing but anger that such filthy scum should attempt to destabilise society's foundations, so the knowledge that there was no release for this soul from the shit he so deserved, came as a relief. Anger soon turned to pain when Virgil pointed out the bald head of a man wearing priest's clothes.

'There are many in this sump from a spectrum of churches, but the world has caught very few of these sinners. The one we are approaching now was one of the first priests to be sent to prison for molesting young children. He cannot speak as his wicked tongue has been cut out and his name has also been eradicated. He is known as RC-F2 and I will tell you his story. He worked in a Catholic school for young boys from the ages of nine to thirteen and he used his position of authority to get away with a series of inexcusable offences against his pupils. He made one boy remove his clothes in the chapel confessional and proceeded to beat his bottom with his bare hands. He did the same with another boy in a bathroom at the school. The naked boy was made to stand over the bath with his genitals hanging over the edge while the priest masturbated with one hand and beat the boy's bottom with the other. If a boy was caught reading an apparently unedifying book such as a Marvel comic, he would be selected by the priest, beaten and sexually abused. He was not in prison for long, but this prison will house him for more time than humans can measure.'

I let out my grievances in a rant. 'People of the church, do you realise how particularly wretched your transgressions are? It is your mission, one you have gladly accepted, to guide people spiritually through life's ups and downs. If you are so weak that you lose sight of your calling then you are not worthy of the privilege God has granted you. It is a shame that you don't die before your time, because it seems the world is waiting to clean up your mess. And what a shitload of mess you will die to!'

Virgil seemed pleased with my candid speech as he listened attentively and smiled. He took me by the hand and led me away from that ditch. As the moon was already low in the sky, it would be daybreak soon, so we needed to get going.

CANTO 24

Counterfeiters

Chained on the Ground under Raining Money

The sinners in the fifth ditch have dared to impersonate other people in order to trick the public or companies out of money. Their obsession with money results in them being forced to sit cross-legged on rugged grey slate, their eyes glued on a moneybag hanging round their neck while bills of money rain down from the sky all around them. Bored demons supervising the immobile souls play a game resembling lacrosse with their pitchforks, but it soon gets nasty.

The counterfeiters

By now I was ready to see what lay in the depth of the next ditch which was sodden with miserable tears. Groups of souls sat cross-legged on the rugged slate at the bottom of the ditch, their hands and legs held in manacles like category A prisoners in high security cells. I didn't recognise any of them. Their obsession with money had eradicated their identities and, on their faces, you could only read a uniform expression of greed.

As my eyes followed the direction of each sinner's gaze, I realised that they were fixed on little money bags hanging around their necks. Falling from the grey misty air, like little birds swooping down to the ground, were hundreds upon hundreds of bank notes. The notes rained down on the sinners and would have made them rich except that their hands were tied and there was no use for riches in this pitiable place. Instead, the miserable wretches were forced to see, hear and touch the cause of their downfall for ever.

Walking nonchalantly through the seated sinners were troops of demons carrying pitchforks. Occasionally they paused and whispered with each other in small groups and whenever a sinner's eyes strayed from his moneybag necklace to the falling notes in a sense of hope, greed or insolent rebellion, the demons were ready to poke those eyes with the prongs of their pitchforks.

Virgil explained that this group of sinners had obtained money by deception: some through forgery, others through impersonation. Each moneybag was of a distinct design and, as I looked among them, I was intrigued to see on one of the bags a replica painting of Christ breaking bread at the table with two disciples at Emmaus.

Han van Meegeren

Virgil could see that I wanted to find out more, so he encouraged me to talk to a few of the souls to hear their stories. I squatted down to look more closely at the painting on the moneybag and to get closer to the seated sinner. 'Please tell me who you are and what is the meaning of this painting on which you feast your eyes?'

The sinner reddened and squirmed on his buttocks but without lifting his gaze for fear of being prodded by a watchful demon, he said, 'For many years, I toiled over my creations, but nobody thought anything of them. People criticised me for lacking in originality! Rather than put down my brushes and pack away my easel, I decided to have the last laugh on my insensitive critics. I would ride on the back of the already famous artists by emulating their work and I revelled as well-renowned art critics hailed the newly found masterpieces "What sentiment!"; "What understanding!"; "An example of the highest art!" I then planned to expose their idiocy by revealing that the paintings were in fact hoaxes.'

'Tell me, how did you fool so many historians and critics in the art world? People often retell stories of old in a new and different way, and I myself have been known to retell classical stories, but I would never claim to be an Ovid or a Homer!'

'You are lucky that people rate you for who you are. I only found my acceptance in the world by fooling the critics who tried to erase me. People loved my work, and I made my fortune by forging works by a painter the world will come to know as Vermeer, along with works by many other Old Dutch Masters. I took great care to use the canvas, materials and paint pigments of the time and I used a special hardening substance which, when baked, hardened the paint rock solid giving it the appearance of being hundreds of years old. They fell for it hook, line and sinker. They were so convinced that I decided not to reveal the hoaxes but instead kept on crafting new forgeries. Only when I was arrested for selling a Vermeer to the Nazis, in what was seen as an act of collaboration, did I tell the truth that it was a hoax. God knew the truth of course as here I am amongst the counterfeiters, rather than freezing in the icy ninth circle with the traitors.'

FWA

In another group of manacled sinners, I saw one whose moneybag depicted a piece of paper like a bank note but with a signature written across it at the bottom and the number "100,000" written across the middle.

I asked the soul to tell me who he was and, although he was reluctant to reveal his identity, he explained, 'I made my name forging and faking what the world will come to know as cheques. These are methods of payment to banks, businesses or individuals in return for goods and services. By forging cheques, you could get money out of banks or buy holidays or belongings with no money passing hands at all. I defrauded people by pretending to be a lawyer, then a prison officer, then a pilot who flies vehicles in the air which will be called planes and finally, I pretended to be a security guard. Once I saw how businesses left their daily takings of money in a collection box at their offices. I put a sign on the collection box which read "Out of service. Place deposits with security guard on duty." People handed me wads of money straight into my hands!'

I scorned him, 'You think you are clever, but you can't get your hands on the wads of money falling out of the sky now, can you? You didn't deserve what you creamed off people in life, but you deserve the denial being served up to you in this dingy ditch.'

Playful demons

Just then, I heard one of the demons call out, 'Ouch, Bendylegs, what do you think you are doing?'

'Come on, Batwings, it's just a joke. These sinners aren't going anywhere fast. Here comes another one!'

Bendylegs had a pile of scrunched up bank notes at his clawed feet and was firing them at Batwings' head one at a time using his pitchfork. Bendylegs called to the other demons standing by, 'Pipi, Strello, Chauve, Souris, you're next, so watch out!' Before long, there was a group of them launching balls of notes at each other. Now Strello was using his pitchfork to defend his head and passed the paper ball back to Pipi. Chauve hit a high one at Souris who almost lost his balance as he reached up his pitchfork to deflect the flying object.

Mary Butterworth

It wasn't long before money balls were flying in every direction and, predictably enough, one came hurtling off Chauve's pitchfork and slammed straight into the back of the head of one of the miserable souls sitting within range of the game.

'Hey, what have I done wrong? I am keeping to my side of the bargain, so you should be sticking to yours.' As the soul said this, she turned her head round to look at Chauve, who had caused the injury. The wicked demon responded by bringing down his pitchfork and poking out her eyes.

'Your eyes are of no use to you now that you are no longer crafting forgeries with your quill!' Chauve shouted vindictively.

The sinner had an image of a quill and a pot of ink depicted on her moneybag. I asked her to explain what had brought her to such a low place.

'My name is Mary Butterworth, and I was better than all the other counterfeiters. They used copper plates to forge their notes which were easily found by the authorities who searched suspected houses, and they didn't even produce convincing forgeries. Using the ingenuity of a woman, I devised a system whereby I would iron a piece of muslin over the note that I was aiming to forge in order to transfer the printed shapes. I then covered the muslin with a blank piece of paper and ironed again. The ink came across onto the paper pretty well and the rest I carefully filled in by hand, using ink on my quill pen.' She then fell silent, and her head dropped back down to return her gaze to her moneybag with now empty eyes.

Pimps and Child Groomers

Whipped by Demons

The pimps and child groomers are placed together because they both exploit the desire of others for personal gain. They use and abuse other people sexually for money. They find themselves in the sixth ditch driven and scourged by demons just as they drove others to serve them in life.

Pimps

We moved on from one bridge to the next, chatting about things which don't need to be noted here. We stopped in the middle of the sixth bridge and, looking over the right-hand side, I saw a new shocking scene unfold. The ditch was crammed with souls and, interspersed with the shadowy flesh, were hairy, black demons wielding whips. We slithered down the side of the bridge onto the first bank to get a better look at the horrors held captive here. We turned to the right and followed the edge of the rocky bank above the ditch. Along the bottom of the ditch, I could see two columns of naked sinners. One column was walking towards us and the other was walking in the same direction as us, although their pace was significantly quicker than ours. They resembled queues of people waiting their turn to go into a shop in a time of rations or pandemic, a steady stream of people going in on one side and a steady stream coming out on the other.

Stationed on both sides up on the dark rock like sentries were horned demons with enormous whips, cruelly beating the souls from behind. You should have seen how those souls lifted their legs and danced at the first strike! Nobody wanted to hang around to receive a second or third blow.

Madame Claude

As I was going along, one of the souls caught my eye. She was naked but for a pearl necklace and a pair of pearl earrings. Virgil stopped with me and let me retrace my steps to catch up with her. The whipped soul held her head low, trying to avoid attention but it was too late to hide, and I called out, 'Your pearls give you away in this place where everybody would prefer to bury themselves away. Tell me who you are and what has brought you to this place of suffering.'

'I really don't want to tell you. Remembering the glamour which I enjoyed in life only intensifies the dreariness of this dreadful place. The only spice we can expect in this ditch is the strike of the popper as the demons' whips slice through our flesh. For years, I ran a sex house in Paris serving the rich and famous from all over the world. I employed beautiful, sophisticated girls and matched them carefully with my clients. People dining in the best restaurants around might spot a smartly dressed girl and recognise her as one of my "Claudettes". My clients were presidents, ambassadors and scions of industry and business. My trade was built for the elite. The world will come to recognise the names of the Shah of Iran, John F Kennedy and Gianni Agnelli, to name but a few. I am proud of the fact that I married many of my swans off to rich, important men bringing them a taste of lasting stability in their lives. It is a shame that I haven't achieved such long-lasting pleasure for myself. The only permanence I have is this humiliating, naked state and the unrelenting whipping.'

As she finished talking, a demon struck her with his leather lash and said, 'Push off, pimp! No "Claudettes" to trade here.'

Iceberg Slim

I ran back to catch up with my guide and noticed a tall, slim, soul who seemed unaffected by the lashes the demons unleashed on the processing crowd. Virgil noted what had caught my attention and said, 'Isn't it amazing how he can still hold himself so tall despite the pain afflicted on him and he doesn't even weep? Ask him to tell you his story.'

Without the slightest flinch as the whip cut into his skin, the soul responded to my prompt for information. 'I am known as Iceberg Slim and I controlled a stable of women whom I sold for sex. I was cool as ice in life and haven't changed in death. I needed to keep myself at a distance to preserve my authority, so I cultivated a frosty exterior. It lasted as long as I wasn't sent into a rage by one of my women, in which case, I beat them with whatever crude instrument I had to hand, like clothes hangers. You can tell the world about me and let them know that I wrote it all down in a book called "Pimp: The story of my life." I do not seek to glamorise to the world of pimping. On the contrary, I am sorry for the life I chose, and I want to expose the dehumanising brutality of the industry. It started with a hatred of my mother who let a babysitter sexually abused me as a child. I blamed her and from there, I blamed all women. I read books about psychological manipulation and I pimped to subjugate women using the lessons I had learned. I know that my actions were based on misplaced hatred and what saved me was my mother's unconditional love for me. As a black man who abused and sold black women for sex, I should call myself a counter-revolutionary. I know that the real champions and heroes of the black race are people like the Black Panthers, people who protect them and promote equal opportunities, rather than trash those opportunities as I did.'

'I can see that you made some bad choices which have hurt the most vulnerable people of your time. And they were the very people you should have been standing up for. You may not show any pain on your face, but your heart and soul will be feeling it and when, on Judgement Day, you are reunited with your body, that pain will only intensify and even you will grimace and grieve.' Then I left him to his mental manipulations.

Now we had come right round to the point where the stone bridge jutted out from the rocky bank again. It was a fairly easy climb back over the jagged ledge up to the bridge, and as we crossed the bridge, we made to leave the circling souls to their eternity.

Child groomers

Just at the mid-point of the bridge, Virgil invited me to stop for a moment so that we could see the faces of the second column of sinners. We hadn't been able to see these ones properly before, as they had been travelling in the same direction as us.

I was horrified when Virgil pointed out a group of nine men who had committed grooming offences on girls as young as thirteen. He told me that they would prey on girls in takeaway food shops. One man would lure them in with kind words and gifts and the girls would be sent to different houses for sex. They were frequently raped by much older men. Sometimes a number of girls would be recruited and they would be forced to have sex with a group of men simultaneously or else have sex with up to five men in a day, several times a week. The grooming gang would be paid for the services offered. The gangs were difficult to break as the young victims were rarely believed if they informed the authorities. But none of those sick men escaped divine justice. They are all scourged here, and the world will know all about it.

CANTO 26

Money Launderers

Wearing Leaden Cloaks

In the seventh ditch of Evil Pits, souls who have hidden illegal profits are punished. They are obliged to wear cloaks covered in dazzling gold to represent the money they have made, but the cloaks are made of lead which bears down on the sinners, reflecting their inability to make any spiritual progress.

The money launderers

In the seventh ditch, we found a brightly coloured troop who, in contrast to the last, were going along at a very slow pace. Tears streamed down their faces. They looked feeble and faint. On their backs they wore long cloaks with hoods drawn low over their eyes like Benedictine monks. Their golden exterior was dazzling to the eyes but the cloaks were lined with heavy lead. King Frederick II was well known for making traitors wear lead clothing before tossing them into a boiling cauldron to burn. I can assure you that those garments would have been as light as feathers in comparison to these. What a heavy burden to bear for eternity!

Having crossed the bridge, we turned to the left along the bank and walked with the suffering souls who were pouring out their wretched tears. However, they were so crushed by their burdens that they traipsed at a snail's pace and we were amongst new souls at every step.

Al Capone

Virgil told me that the sinners in this ditch had all been involved in criminal business and that they had hidden the profits made from their shady financial dealings in order to cover their tracks.

'Do you think there is anyone here from my country, Italy?' I asked, looking around at the funereal marching souls.

One of them recognised my accent and called from behind us: "Hey! Hold on a moment. I am from your country, but who are you and how are you able to run so quickly through these murky shadows? I will tell you my story if you will hear it."

Virgil directed me to wait for the soul and then walk along with him. I came to a halt and turned to look at the soul who had addressed me. I could tell that he was willing himself on to reach me as quickly as he could, but his heavy load and the narrow path made it tough going.

When he finally reached us, he strained his eyes around his heavy hood and gazed up at me for a while in silence. Then he spoke again, 'You speak and breathe as if you are alive, and yet, if you are dead, how on earth have you got away without having to wear a leaden robe? Fellow Italian, please tell me who you are and what brings you to this community of miserable money launderers.'

I told the soul, 'I was born and raised on the beautiful river Arno in Florence and I am still alive and kicking. I have been brought here by my honourable guide in order to learn about the sins of the past, present and future and to find a path to happiness and peace on earth. Now tell me who you are with all that grief which pours in torrents down your cheeks? And what is your guilt which glitters and gleams on your shoulders?'

He told me, 'These golden cloaks are made with such thick lead that we groan under the weight like donkeys saddled with heavy weaponry. I am Al Capone, and I am suffering for my years of crime as a gangster. My Italian parents, whom I loved dearly, came to a country, which will come to be known as America, in order to make a new and better life for their family. I grew up at a time when America was going through a period of social reform. Politicians blamed excessive alcohol consumption for high levels of liver disease, drunken behaviour, street crime, absenteeism at work and general social disorder. With Prohibition, there was a nationwide constitutional ban on the manufacture and sale of alcohol. As a result, opportunities opened up for black market trading and I leapt at the chance to earn a quick buck. My challenge was to hide the profits which were coming in thick and fast. I needed a cash business to bury my illegal earnings and I chose to buy up a number of laundry shops. People would pay cash to wash their clothes and without invoices to evidence transactions, there was no paper trail. I slipped the liquor revenue into the tills. Ker-ching! They were incredibly profitable laundry businesses by all accounts.

'I need the world to know that I wasn't all bad. I gave a lot of money to charities over the years and people liked the fact that I was what the world will come to know as a Robin Hood character. I robbed the rich to give to the poor. But luck never lasts forever, and the authorities came after me for tax evasion. Do you think the government should receive tax on goods which they themselves have made illegal? You can make your own judgement as the earthly judges did for me, but, as you can see, divine judgement has me suffering eternally for hiding those ill-gotten gains and polluting the world's finances.'

I thought about the question Al Capone had raised and the gap between earthly and divine judgement. Justice systems create laws designed to govern our society, but the moral code governs the decisions we make for good or ill. While the former is fundamental to a cohesive and well-functioning society in life, the latter is fundamental to what happens after death. Lying or passing on information which a friend has told you in confidence will not break any laws, but I had already observed the consequences of lying and cheating in the eighth circle of Hell.

Al Capone told me about other money launderers weighed down in his ditch and pointed out banking executives from Danske Bank. He explained that Danske was Denmark's largest lending bank and, when it acquired a branch in Estonia, a series of suspiciously large transactions coming from Russia were flagged up. The company kept doing business with Russia because they were enjoying high levels of profit, but soon, almost all of the Estonian branch's profits came from people living in Russia or countries which were once part of Russia. The bank was fined by international authorities and the executive decision-makers are forever reminded that they siphoned dirty money into the world as they struggle under the weight of their leaden guilt.

In another group, Al Capone showed me souls who had profited from money laundering at an American bank called Wachovia. This bank wanted to make money out of South American countries and processed large transactions which originated from the drugs industry through foreign exchange kiosks. The drug dealers would hand cash to the foreign exchange kiosk which would issue a bill for the drug dealers to get clean foreign currency from the bank.

One of the money launderers told us about his life on the road. 'I had no wife or children. There was nothing normal about my life. I spent a lot of time travelling between tax havens in the Caribbean and Europe. Normal people go home at the end of the day and have dinner with their family. They are off duty. Money laundering means you are never off duty. You could be called at any time of the day or night by a client needing to get rid of cash covertly and at speed. I've been there. I've seen it. If I'd known this is where I'd end up, I'd have stuck to the day job. Nothing is done at speed here. There are hundreds of sinners in this ditch, hiding under their hoods and weighed down by these cloaks of sin.'

I could see that the law was successful in protecting the public up to a point, but the comprehensive punishment of these sinners was plain for me to see in this profit-stained pit.

Blackmailers and Extortionists

Suffering Disease and Pestilence

The eighth ditch contains blackmailers and extortionists. They use threats or deception to elicit goods or money from innocent people, distorting the very commodities on which society lives to survive: money, food and medicines. It is the image of a diseased society and these souls pay the price in fever, flesh-eating diseases and putrefaction.

Blackmailers and extortionists

Virgil had already set off and I had no choice but to follow him. 'You may have heard about things in the Evil Pits of fraud which you don't fully understand as society and practices will change considerably over time. There will be significant human progress in labour, travel and communication but, as long as you grasp the fundamentals of the sins which have brought these souls to their place in Hell, you will be surprised just how little human failings have changed. It is enough that you record what you have seen and tell the world so that future generations can be forewarned of the consequences of their decisions.'

We carried on talking until we reached the point on the bridge which gave us a view of the next ditch, or it would have done had there been enough light to enable us to penetrate the damp, dark and fetid air. Terrifying wails of lament echoed in the darkness. Their reverberations pummelled our senses with pelts of pity and I had to put my hands over my ears for the sake of my sanity. There was as much pain and sorrow in this ditch as if you had gathered all the sick people ridden with fever, plague and disease and dropped them into this sickbay. The stink of rotting flesh made you want to retch.

We descended onto the bank keeping to the left-hand side. As I drew closer to the edge of the ditch, the view to the base became clearer. Here, the High Lord's minister, Infallible Justice, punished the blackmailers who are registered within.

It was shocking to behold the multitudes of languishing souls heaped up in piles of rotting flesh in this dingy ditch. It was even worse than the sorrow on the Greek island of Aegina during the plague when you could taste sickness in the air and all the beasts, even the littlest worm, dropped dead.

Some lay flopped on top of each other, shoulder to foot, belly to arm. Others dragged their sluggish limbs on all fours along the dismal path. Step by step, we inched forwards in silence, watching and hearing the plaints of these souls who could barely lift their bodies from the ground.

Virgil watched me turn green in the face and said, 'The world will come to know about plagues, pestilence, fast-spreading flus and coronavirus pandemics. They are earthly diseases which affect both good people and bad, but these blackmailing sinners will be tormented by ill health for eternity. They have forced innocent people to hand over money or goods by threatening them or by falsely earning their trust. Take moral strength as your medicine. They do not deserve your pity.'

I was curious to understand the nature of this sin, and asked Virgil to tell me more. 'You will have met greedy landlords who charge farmers excessive rents to work their land. When the poor farmer has run out of money, the landlord demands livestock and produce worth far more than value of the rent due. Then you will hear of gangs who patrol the fields demanding payment from farmers for protection from thieves. These rackets are the purest form of fraud and people who make these choices are as sick in the head as the oozing scabs you see before you.'

Charles Ponzi and Bernie Madoff

I saw two souls covered from head to toe in scabs and propped up against each other, back-to-back like filled Christmas stockings warming by the fire. The souls furiously scratched and scraped at their own flesh to kill the irrepressible itch that consumed them. They dragged their nails down over their scabs like a fisherman's knife scrapes the scales off a sea bream.

Virgil turned to one of the souls and said, 'I hope your nails are up to the job as you rip and tear at yourselves for eternity!'

One of them replied, weeping, 'I am Charles Ponzi and if I have judged your accent correctly, you are Italian like me. Like many other Italians of my time, I went to America to seek a fortune and make my family rich. I am afraid I didn't do any credit to our homeland as I will be known to the world as the person who defrauded thousands of people out of their investments. If you had met me in life, you wouldn't recognise me now that I am so hideously deformed. But who are you and why are you so interested?'

Virgil explained, 'I am guiding this living man from ditch to ditch through the abyss, and I am destined to show him the whole of Hell.'

The stunned pair broke apart from each other and, trembling nervously in confusion, they turned to stare at me along with scores of others who had heard my guide's words echo down the ditch.

Virgil drew close to me and said, 'Ask them whatever you want.'

Encouraged by his words, I began, 'If there is anything good which you can tell me of yourselves, now is your chance, so people can remember your stories for years to come. Don't let the shame of your frightful punishment stop you from talking to me.'

'Well, I did make quite a few investors rich. The early ones at least. I was offering interest rates at hundred percent after ninety days or fifty percent after forty-five days compared with bank deposit returns of only five percent. The numbers looked amazing and it didn't take much sweet talking to convince people to invest. I paid earlier investors' returns out of the new investments, and new investors just continued to come knocking at my door. I enjoyed a lavish lifestyle, but I did give generously to charity too. However, when the authorities started to question my stellar profits given my humble beginnings, the penny dropped. As soon as the investments dried up, I defaulted on the interest payments and the banks I had deposited investments with also collapsed. A lot of investors never saw their money again. Here I am with Bernie Madoff who imitated my scheme and defrauded people of even more money with his false promises of consistently high returns.'

The Wolf of the High Street

As he finished speaking, a pair of naked souls came charging towards us like terriers let loose from their cage, threatening to bite anything that comes across their path. One of them pounced on Charles Ponzi and tore into his neck with his teeth. Then it dragged him, scraping his scabby front along the stony track. Bernie was left behind, trembling at the thought that he may be next in line, and said, 'That pixie who rabidly bites anything he sees is the Wolf of the High Street who manipulated stocks to increase in price and then sold them at inflated prices. The other scampering soul is Kim Woo-choong, who exploded his conglomerate, Daewoo, with huge amounts of debt. He tried to manipulate the share price to offset the debt burden, but the global economic crisis sent the company spiralling into bankruptcy. You see, the unrelenting justice which torments us here balances the books.'

I kept my eyes fixed keenly on those two raging souls and only once they had passed did I turn to look at the other damned souls. I saw one shaped like a lute – if you can imagine a body without his legs. It looked as though he had terrible oedema bloating and swelling the stomach and leaving the head, neck and chest looking long and thin like the handle of the instrument. His parched lips were curled open like a patient with a hot fever who craves water.

'I can see you passing through this wicked place apparently without punishment although I can't imagine why. Look at the misery piled on me,

Farmer B. I used to farm dairy cows for their milk but now I am gasping for a single drop of water. I can't stop thinking about the clear, cool streams which would run off the green fields to give my cows drinking water. The thought of that distant, cool water is punishment enough but this disease really ravages my features. I wanted more money for my pints of milk, so I hid shards of metal in jars of baby food on the shops' shelves and told the shop owners they'd need to pay me millions to be told which jars were contaminated.'

I was appalled by this story of extortion and wilful harm to innocent babies. 'You deserve to suffer the thirst which cracks your tongue and the foul water which bloats your belly so much so that you can't even see your toes!'

CANTO 28

The Evil Claws

The human traffickers and people smugglers are plunged in boiling tar and taunted by a band of arrogant, punchy demons called the Evil Claws. The traffickers have a blatant disregard for human rights as they sell people for slavery or sex while the people smugglers take money for facilitating illegal immigration often in unseaworthy vessels. All these crimes feed on poverty, social inequality and vulnerability. The sinners are punished by being submerged in a hellish version of the oceans or terrain which they moved people across.

The ninth ditch

We made our way along the rocky path until we arrived at the buttress for the next bridge. From there we stopped to look into the ninth ditch of Evil Pits and the next hopeless expression of suffering, but it was getting increasingly difficult to see through the darkness.

The scene which unfolded in the murky fog below was like a Venetian shipyard. There the shipbuilders busy themselves boiling thick sticky tar which they use to fix their vessels in the winter months when the boats are off the water. Imagine a hive of activity with new ships being built and older boats being repaired and reconditioned. Imagine the sounds. The hammer strikes its blows and the chisel files and scrapes; carpenters sculpt new oars; braiders twist rope; and sailmakers mend rips and tears.

Here the tool of torment was not fire, shit, lead or slicing swords, but hot tar which bubbled up from the bottom of the ditch and covered the banks in black glue. This much I could see, but I could see nothing else. I got the sense of a seething mass of black bubbles which heaved to the surface, swelling up and then back down again.

While I was staring in amazement at the latest torture chamber, Virgil called urgently, 'Watch out! Mind yourself!' and he pulled me over towards him. My eagerness to turn and look at what he was pointing out was tempered by hesitance, as I was afraid at what I might see. There was no escaping because right behind us came a black demon running along the rocky edge of the bridge. I can't tell you how ferocious and fierce he seemed with his outstretched wings and lightning speed. He was gripping the scrawny ankles of a sinner slung over his bony shoulder.

He pulled up a short distance from us on the bridge and called down to his comrades who were hidden under the arches, 'Hey fellow Evil Claws! I have got a coyote here from Mexico! Push him under with your pitchfork and I'll head back to fetch another one. There are plenty more to come and they're all profiteering from inequality. Oh, I forgot to mention José Louis and his gang. He was the worst of the lot, selling Mexican boys and girls as slaves to work in the richer north of America. He sent them across in the back of dirty old trucks with no food for days.'

He hurled the soul into the ditch and turned back on the rocky ridge as fast as a policeman in pursuit of a thief.

The Evil Claws

The sinner sank and came back to the surface writhing in pain. The band of demons hidden under the bridge shouted, 'Your prayers for help aren't going to help you now. This is not a day out at the beach at Cancun! If you don't want to be forked, then stay under where we can't see you!'

More than a hundred prongs were raised at the ready to stab him back down. The Evil Claws taunted him, 'Get your squirming body under and do your dark deals where you can hide.' They were like cooks pushing morsels of meat down into the stew with their forks.

Virgil meets Evil Tail

It was clear that these spirited demons were not to be trusted and we'd had our fair share of provocations with this evil breed. Virgil took control as always, saying, 'You are going to have to hide yourself, so squat down behind this boulder where no one can see you. Whatever happens, don't worry as I know exactly what these demons are like and have faced off their type before.'

Memories of the dreadful demons at the gates of Discord unsettled me, but Virgil seemed confident that he could handle this boisterous brigade. He continued over the bridge and, as he reached the edge of the ninth ditch, I'd say he needed all the confidence he could muster.

The demons came running out from under the bridge like dogs goaded on by the pack to pounce on their prey. They raised their pitchforks in the air pointing them towards him, but he cried, 'Hold back your forks! Before you poke me, I would like to talk with one of you and then you can decide whether I am someone who needs poking.'

They shouted in unison, 'Go on Evil Tail!'

Then one of the evil pack came forward, grumbling under his breath, 'What's the bloody point?' The others, all the while, remained rooted to the ground.

Virgil called out, 'Come on, Evil Tail, do you really think I could make it this far through Hell without divine will and providence? I have been given a mission to guide another being along this wild path, so let us pass.'

His pride was so knocked on hearing these words that he let his pitchfork drop by his side and said to the others, 'Looks like we'll 'ave to let 'im off then.'

Virgil turned to me and said, 'No need to stay crouched behind that rock anymore. It's safe to come out now.' Relieved at this outcome, I quickly ran out to join him, but the demons all pressed towards us again and I really didn't trust them.

I huddled right up to my guide and didn't take my eyes off the demons who continued to look at us threateningly. They lowered their pitchforks and murmured amongst themselves. 'Shall I give him what for?' one of them urged.

'Yeah, go get him on the butt!'

But the demon who had spoken with Virgil turned angrily on his trooper saying, 'Leave it out, Roughface!'

Then he spoke to us. 'You can't go any further on this 'ere cliff path as the bridge over the final ditch in Evil Pits has collapsed into rubble. If you want to get out of 'ere any time soon, you'll need to follow the edge of the ditch till you find another bridge further on. The bridge broke in an almighty earthquake all those years ago when Christ was crucified. I am sending some of my men down that way to watch for any souls who try to come up for air. You can go with 'em if you like and they won't hurt you.'

The patrol of demons

Then Evil Tail called to his men, 'I need Bendywings, Frostyfeet and Bigdog! Curlybeard, you can be patrol leader. Windcheater, you can come too, along with Dragonface. I'll 'ave Boarhead with your tusks, Scratchclaws, Fleaface and crazy Redhead. Watch closely over the boiling black, and make sure these two 'ere get safely to the next bridge which'll get 'em over the ditch.'

I didn't like the sound of it. 'Oh no, I don't think so. I trust you, Virgil, but not this lot. Why do we need an escort when you know your way? You are usually good at sensing things around you. Can't you see their grinding teeth and threatening frowns?'

'Look, don't worry', Virgil reassured me. 'They aren't beating their brows at us, but at the wretched sinners.'

The demons wheeled round on the left bank but, before they set off, they signalled to the patrol leader by sticking out their tongues and he responded with a flabby fart.

Human Traffickers and Smugglers

Submerged in Boiling Tar

As the evil demons spar amongst themselves, we see how Hell has no true order and is divided against itself. In this place, fear is the only discipline. Moreover, the devil is a fool as trickery plays on trickery and cruelty on cruelty.

The demons, the traffickers and the smugglers

Well, I can honestly say that I have never seen troops called to arms by such a signal as that flabby fart! At Virgil's prompting, I went along with the ten demons despite feeling terrified in their company. I reasoned that we were on their patch, so we had to go along with their ways. Each to their own I suppose.

My attention was fully focused on the gooey tar and I was watching out for the souls who were boiling in it. Like dolphins who send signals to sailors that a storm is coming by bringing the arch of their back to the surface, so these sinners would occasionally bring their backs to the surface to alleviate their pain, and then plunge back down quick as lightning to hide themselves.

Other sinners hovered at the edge like frogs in the shallows of a pond poking the tips of their nostrils out of the water. But when Curlybeard approached them, they'd slither back into the bubbling black broth.

Snakehead

The thought still makes me shudder, but I saw a soul waiting at the edge hoping for some temporary relief, when Scratchclaws, who was the closest, hooked his tarred locks and dragged him out, squirming like a just-landed salmon.

I listened in to the demons' taunts as they shouted, 'Hey, Redhead, make sure you stick your claws in deep and rip him open!'

I turned to my guide. 'Can we find out who that unlucky criminal is they have just captured?'

Virgil approached the wriggling wretch and asked him where he'd come from. 'I am known as Snakehead, and I am paying a hot price for smuggling people from Africa to Europe. I faked documents to get them into new countries and piled them onto old inflatable dinghies. I smuggled twenty-five people when the boat only accommodated twelve, so many lives were lost at sea. I made sure I got paid well before I sent them to their deaths. Women, children and babies too. They simply wanted a better life than the one they were leaving at home, but this eternal drowning is my just reward.'

Then Boarhead, who had a lethal tusk protruding from either side of his mouth, leant in to show him just how cleanly they could cut. The cats were certainly amongst the pigeons now but Curlybeard held him in an armlock and said, 'Stay back while I grab him with my pitchfork.'

He then turned to Virgil saying, 'If you are still interested, ask him your question before he gets mashed.'

Virgil took the opportunity to ask, 'Can you tell us about the other sinners submerged in this black tar?'

'Just a moment ago, I was sinking in the mire with a Nigerian soul who trafficked girls to Gabon for domestic servitude and prostitution. Despite his crimes, I wish I was still submerged as I'd be out of reach of claws and hooks!'

Windcheater chimed in, 'Right, that's quite enough!' and he drove his pitchfork into Snakehead's arm, slicing it open to reveal a scrawny sinew. Dragonface stepped forward too, plunging a pitchfork into the soul's legs when their patrol leader, Curlybeard, swung round with a chiding look.

When they had all calmed down a little, Virgil took the opportunity to prod further. He asked Snakehead, who was still gazing at his injury in disbelief, to tell us more about the other sinners here. The hooked soul sighed and said, 'There are souls from countries all across the world such as Columbia and Egypt, as well as China and India. Like me, they profit from smuggling people who are desperate for higher wages in countries like America and western Europe. But, oh no, here comes another demon gnashing his teeth! I would talk more but I am afraid he'll have my hide!'

The great commander turned to Fleaface, who was about to explode with the urge to stab, and said, 'Out of the way, you hideous hairy hawk!'

The terrified soul croaked, 'If you want to meet some more sinners, I'll send them to you. If the Evil Claws put down their weapons for a while, the souls won't be afraid to show themselves. For one of me, I'll send you seven more who'll be summoned by my special whistle.'

Hearing this, Bigdog lifted his muzzle and shook his head. 'Did you hear how he's trying to trick us for a way to escape our claws?'

And as Snakehead wasn't short of a trick or two, he said, 'Yes, I am the artful dodger and watch me dodge your blows by luring my fellows into your evil hands instead of me!'

Bendywings couldn't stand it any longer and burst out, 'If you dive back down, I may not be able to chase you on foot, but I do have wings to beat you with. We'll hide below the edge of the bank so you can't see us and then we'll see whose tricks are best! It's ten against one!'

Now, dear reader, get ready for another game. The whole patrol of demons turned to hide on the other side of the bank. Snakehead waited for his moment and when their backs were turned, he sprang up and dived back into the boiling tar. The demons were smarting with rage, and Bendywings felt it the most keenly, as it was his boast that had been trumped. He cried, 'Right, you rascal! Got you now!' But to no avail. The demon's wings couldn't fly as fast as fear. The sinner plunged under, and the demon flew up and over, failing to get close. Frostyfeet was furious they had been foiled and flew after Bendywings, hoping that the sinner would keep out of the way so he could fight it out with his comrade. As soon as the soul had disappeared under the brewing squelch, Frostyfeet dug his claws into his fellow fiend, and they grappled in a tussle above the ditch. But Bendywings gave him his best and, tossing and turning, they both fell into the scorching sticky squelch below. The heat immediately unlocked their embrace but escape they couldn't. Their wings were glued fast in the tar.

Curlybeard, cursing madly with the rest of them, sent four demons to the other bank with pitchforks in hand. So now, from both sides of the ditch, the troop swept the squelch to fish out those unfortunate pirates who by now were cooked beneath the crust. And there we left them to their chaos and confusion.

CANTO 30

Corrupt Public Officials

Plunged Headfirst into Holes with Flames Licking the Soles of their Feet

Dante and Virgil find a moment to bond after the demons' pranks and before the ultimate evil is revealed at the core of Hell. In the final ditch of Evil Pits, they meet corrupt officials from the government and from the church. In medieval times, religious powers frequently crossed the line into the more traditional and rightfully held powers of the State. Corruption within the institutions of government and the church contributes to political and social divisions. It erodes public trust and, at its worst, can lead to anarchy. These persistent problems highlight the need for reform today just as it did in thirteenth century Italy.

Dante and Virgil flee

Silent, alone and without escort, we continued our journey one in front of the other, like processing monks. As I dwelt on the tiff we had just witnessed, I thought of Aesop's fable, the one about the frog and the mouse. As Mouse went about the fields, he came across a stream with a number of frogs croaking away. Mouse was unsure how he was going to get across when Frog came out towards him thinking he'd make a tasty breakfast. Putting on his charm, Frog pretended to want to help Mouse saying, 'Wrap your leg around mine and you won't fall in.' Trusting Frog, Mouse got on and they got as far as the middle of the stream when Frog tried to draw Mouse under the water and drown him. Mouse spread himself out to keep himself afloat when a hawk flying above noticed Mouse and swooped down to take him. But Frog was still attached to Mouse's leg, so the hawk gobbled up the pair of them.

Frostyfeet deceived Bendywings by pretending he'd set off to help his comrade but, actually, he was after a fight and, in the end, they both ended up in the slurry.

One thought led to another, and then I became doubly doubtful. I was thinking that if the demons had been tricked and humiliated because of us, then they would be even more angry than usual. Stoked by their wicked spite, they were sure to come after us like dogs after a hare.

I felt the hairs on the back of my neck bristle from fear as I pondered what was behind us, and I whispered to Virgil, 'Quickly, you need to find us a hiding spot as the Evil Claws are coming after us. I am terrified. I am sure I can already hear them.'

'Listen, I have come up with a plan. If there's a slope on the right-hand side over there which'll get us down to the next ditch, we can escape the dangerous demons who are hot on our heels.'

He had barely finished telling me his plan, when I saw the demons swooping down towards us, their wings outstretched and their claws poised to grab us.

Virgil immediately picked me up in his arms like a mother protecting her baby from imminent danger, and he fled headlong over the rocky edge sliding down the jagged slope which bordered the next ditch. You have never seen water from a fountain gush so eagerly into the pool as my guide ran down that steep bank carrying me close to his chest, not like a companion but more like a son. His feet had scarcely touched the bottom of the ditch when the demons arrived on the ridge right above us. We weren't worried by now, though, as Providence on high, which gives the Evil Claws guardianship of the ninth moat, confines their power to that territory, thereby fencing their evil tricks in.

The climb onto the final bank

We still needed to get out of the ditch on the other side in order to make it to the safety of the far bank, and, this time, Providence was close at hand. A little further on, we saw fallen rocks from the broken bridge which would allow us to scramble up onto the bank where we were headed.

Virgil was cross that Evil Tail had fibbed about the second bridge which clearly didn't exist. 'The devil has many vices, and he is the father of all lies!'

I felt disheartened seeing my guide so troubled, but he was quick to reassume authority. As we came to the ruined bridge, Virgil turned to me with the kind and gentle smile I recognised from before, at the foot of the mountain. He surveyed the ruin carefully, and then he opened his arms and lifted me up to help me climb the rocky face. Like a good workman who checks and plans things out ahead, he helped me up onto one crag and looking up for the next foothold, he said, 'Right, that one next. Now, pull yourself up onto that rock, but make sure it can take your weight first.'

Thank goodness the slope on this side of the ditch was shorter than on the opposite bank where we had slithered down. I don't know about my guide, but that would have finished me off. The abyss narrows to its deepest point so each ditch in Evil Pits gets smaller and smaller and each bank is lower than the preceding one. Finally, we reached the top of the rockfall, but my heart was pounding. I was so exhausted, that I couldn't move any further and had to sit down to catch my breath.

Virgil did the talking. 'It takes hard work and dedication to achieve progress and happiness and leave your mark in life. If you sit on a bed of feathers or hide under your duvet, you will leave nothing of note on this earth. Your life will be forgotten like a puff of smoke. So, up you get, and use your inner strength to overcome your fatigue. We aren't finished yet. There are still some tough parts to the journey ahead and getting up that rockfall is just a taster. If you can understand this and put mind over matter, you will reap the rewards.'

I got myself to my feet and tried to make light of my recovery. 'OK let's go. I am ready for this.' We made our way along the rocky ridge which was rugged, narrow and tricky, and much steeper than the previous ridge. I talked as I went in order to disguise any sense of struggle.

Corruption in public office

Now it was the time for corrupt officials to hear the sound of the trumpet calling them to judgement. The sides and bottom of the ditch we now circled were lined with grey stone rather than boiling tar. Perfectly round and equally formed holes studded the stone casing, and from the mouth of each hole, I could see a sinner's feet and legs poking out as far as the calf; but the rest of the body, plunged headfirst into the hole, remained hidden inside. Flames licked the soles of their feet like the flames on a Christmas pudding, making them wriggle and writhe so fast that they might have contended for the hundred metre final.

Pope Nicholas III

'Tell me, who's that tormented wretch wriggling more than the rest of this bunch and who's being scorched by a hotter flame?' I asked my guide.

'If you want, I'll carry you down there by that gentler slope and you can hear the story from the horse's mouth.' Virgil carried me all the way to the sinner's hole where I found him upside down, planted headfirst in the ground like a post. These public officials had abused their position by focusing on material things and on selfish strength and dominance, rather than on their public or spiritual duty to nurture all people equally. They had got it all upside down and were suffering on their heads in death.

I felt like a priest bending down to hear confession when the soul shouted up at me, 'It can't be you, can it? Is that Pope Boniface standing there? The Book of the Future has lied to me by several years if you are already to be plunged into my hole of corruption on account of all that money you pilfered from the church.'

I was dumbstruck and didn't know how to respond until Virgil prompted me, 'Hurry up and explain that you are not at all who he thinks you are!'

As I set the record straight, the spirit wiggled his feet frantically, furious at having given away his identity; and then, sighing and apparently choked up with sorrow, he said, 'So, what do you want? Since you seem so keen to know who I am that you came all the way down here, I will tell you that I was Pope Nicholas III and, wanting to make my family rich, I pocketed money from the church and now I find myself pocketed in this pit dedicated to popes. Beneath my head lie the others, compressed in these rocky crevices, for trading church possessions. I will also be crushed down there when Pope Boniface VIII, the one I rashly thought you were, is plunged on top of me. He won't be planted here for long because the even more stained Pope Clement V will then take his place. That one bribed the king of France to make him pope and then proceeded to make himself a rich man whilst abandoning his flock.'

'Tell me, if you have read the Book of the Future, which other sinners will have their heads planted in holes with fire frying the skin on their feet?' I asked.

'I can tell you names of some of the sinners who are thrust in Hell and what has brought them here. Many are sinners of the future who have abused their positions of power. They have stolen; they have issued favours; they have cheated on their wives; or they have killed or starved many people along the way. The sinners I mention may be here already. I can't see them with my head planted in here, but I can tell you what I've read. They will have their heads buried in these slots like marbles in the devil's own game of solitaire. There is a round hole for every country that exists or will exist in the entire world. Many of them are already filled but I can assure you that there will be plenty more to come as power never ceases to corrupt. You can tell the world about the filth found here and people will remember them by the emblem they are buried with.

'Buried with his black shirt in the hole for Italy, you will find Mussolini who slaughtered thousands in the name of Fascism. He ordered the murder of the anti-fascist politician, Giacomo Matteotti, who threatened to publicise the government's sale of Italian oil rights to an American oil company. Mussolini committed electoral fraud and he had numerous flings and affairs, including with the Belgian princess who was, at the time, married to Italy's last king, Umberto II. The world will easily guess the identity of the next Italian minister to be sucked down here.

'In the hole for France, you will find King Louis XIV holding a golden sun. He had numerous affairs with women, and he used public funds to build the opulent Palais de Versailles. President Mitterand will also be there paying for his infidelities, for associating with Vichy Nazi collaborators and for using public funds to build large monuments in his name such as Bastille-Opéra, the Grande Arche de la Défence and the glass pyramid at the entrance to the Louvre in Paris. He will forever see a reflection of his shame as he will be buried with a replica of the glass pyramid.

'In the hole for Great Britain, you will find King Henry VIII, buried with a church collection plate. He threw out his faithful first wife and outrageously overturned the church in order to marry his lover, Anne Boleyn. There will be Labour minister, John Belcher, with a gift box in his hands. He is to be punished for the lavish gifts he received from the lobbyist Sidney Stanley. In return, he was encouraged to use his position of authority to protect Stanley from the accusation that one of his businesses had breached the paper rationing rules during World War II rationing. There will be Conservative minister, Robert Boothby, holding a picture of young boys and bank notes for his errant ways with sex and gambling. He had an affair with the wife of the Prime Minister in waiting, Harold Macmillan, and he had a close relationship with the gangster Ronnie Kray who pimped him boys for gay sex. There will also be John Profumo, Secretary of State for war, who holds a condom in his hands. He lied about his affair with the prostitute, Christine Keeler, who was linked with a Russian military attaché.

'In the hole for Spain, you will find General Franco holding the flag of Fe-Jons with the red yolk and arrows on a black background. He abused his position through power rather than sex and built concentration camps for large numbers of political prisoners encouraging forced labour. He censured the media, and he repressed the culture of separatist regions of Spain such as Catalonia.

'In the hole for Russia, with his face scarred by smallpox, you will find Stalin. He is punished for using violence to suppress the poor and for shooting down any opposition until he gained absolute power.

'In the hole for Romania, there will be Nicolae Ceau?escu with his long black winter coat. He flooded the police with informants, and dissidents were killed with radiation. He used public funds to build the Palace of Parliament, the second largest building in the world. He censured and controlled the media and he indulged in an opulent lifestyle while many in his country suffered hardships.

'There is a hole for Yugoslavia, a country broken apart by forces no one could control, with Slobodan Milo?evi? planted inside wearing a butcher's apron. He committed electoral fraud, he manipulated the media, and was nicknamed the "Balkan Butcher" for the widespread ethnic cleansing he ordered to shore up his dictatorship.

'In the hole for Chile, you will find Augusto Pinochet holding a piggy bank and a sword for his illegal financial dealings, his human rights abuses and for the tens of thousands of his opponents whom he tortured.

'There is a hole for Uganda containing Idi Amin in his red and green cap. He appointed death squads to rout out opponents who were raped and tortured at will. Bodies were hacked and mutilated or even fed to crocodiles. Political rivals were decapitated. If that wasn't enough to assure him of a spot in the tenth ditch of Evil Pits, he also committed flagrant nepotism and indulged in polygamy to satisfy his sexual appetite.

'In the hole for Zimbabwe, you will find Robert Mugabe with his wide rimmed glasses. He used his power to confiscate farms, he manipulated laws to seize control of foreign and white-owned businesses and he was unfaithful to his wife. He also spent public money on opulent homes and enjoyed a lavish lifestyle when many were struggling to survive.

'Mohamed Suharto will be planted in the hole for Indonesia with his black songkok on his head. He will pay the price for corruption, collusion and nepotism. He killed just short of a million people in an anti-communist purge and he kidnapped and assassinated his government's critics.

'In the China hole, Mao Zedong will be buried with his little red book. He incited peasants to start a revolution in order to assert communist control, and he also starved his country of food in exchange for nuclear weapons. He had serial affairs and sex with dancers and girls on his staff and he owned villas, mountains and lakes while many Chinese people lived in cramped conditions. The book mentions plenty more, but that must give you a flavour of the evil and corruption caused by sex, money and power, the world over.'

I thought back to the soul with the black square of moustache we had met in the seventh circle of the violent. That one held a public office. Why wasn't he down here?

Virgil, who always anticipated my thoughts, explained, 'Where some souls suffer punishment higher up in Hell, it is possible that they have been so evil that divine judgement will make them go through Hell twice. Usually, the souls will be thrown to the circle of their most wicked sin, but exceptions may be made. That soul with the black moustache from the boiling river of blood is bound to find himself in a renewed Hell, as subverted sediment squeezed into these sinkholes.'

I was deeply saddened by so many stories of corrupt and deviant officials. Whether they are leaders in our past or in our future, their role should always be to achieve peace, prosperity and harmony across all classes, races and religions in their own nation. They can only do that if they act as role models earning the public's trust and respect. If our leaders can't abide by respectable standards then either their oppressive dictatorship smashes their people or the system itself blows apart. In both cases, society breaks down and the risk of anarchy ensues. But then I thought back to Pope Nicholas III who had recounted tales of corruption from the Book of the Future. The church was equally important in this debate. People need spiritual guidance just as much as earthly governance, and if our faith is weakened by corruption amongst our church leaders, then happiness on earth as well as in the hereafter will not be possible.

I'm afraid I let out all my anger at Pope Nicholas III when, really, a pope should command the utmost respect. 'Did our Lord demand money or sex from St Peter before giving him the keys to the Church? No, he simply said: "Follow me". You stay right where you. The only person you are following now is the sinful pope buried beneath you and you will find his smelly feet in your nose for eternity. The church should never have crossed the line into matters concerning secular governance. Blame rests with our first Roman emperor, Constantine, who decided to gift Rome to the church. From that point on, spiritual concerns were mingled with the concerns of kings and emperors and look where that has landed us!'

As I ranted on, the pope was bugged by so much anger or self-consciousness that both his feet wriggled and kicked madly around. I am pretty sure Virgil was pleased with my candid speech as he listened attentively and smiled. At this moment, he put both his arms around me, and lifting me to his chest, he made his way back up the way we had come down.

The Giants at the Circle of Treachery; Cocytus

Dante and Virgil have arrived at the well at the bottom of the abyss and there they find giants standing like statues around the rim. These giants are effectively the pillars of Hell and, lacking in reason, intellect or emotion, they are reduced to rock, the very fabric of Hell itself.

The giants

Virgil set me down on that final bridge out of Evil Pits and, feeling restored, I turned my back on that dastardly ditch. Together, we walked to the edge of the shrinking abyss without a word between us.

You couldn't tell whether it was daytime or night-time as the dim light made time uncertain. I couldn't see much, but I could clearly hear the blare of a resounding horn which crashed louder than thunder. My eyes were drawn towards the blast which came from behind us. Its call heralded an event more dreadful than Roland's horn, Olifant, which, blown with his last desperate breath, reached Charlemagne eight miles away and warned of his Christian army's slaughter by the Islamic Saracens.

As I turned in the direction of the noise, I made out a number of tall towers and asked, 'Virgil, what on earth is this city doing here?'

He explained, 'We're too far away to see anything clearly in these dark shadows, so it isn't what you think it is. It will all become clear when we get closer and you will see how you have let your imagination get the better of you. Let's get moving and you'll see.'

Virgil took me lovingly by the hand and said, 'I don't want you to be too shocked when we get there, so I will tell you now that they aren't in fact towers, but giants, standing in the well at the bottom of this abyss. The towers you thought you saw are the giants' bodies, visible from the waist up.'

A I approached the rim of the well, it was like a fog was lifting and I began to see through the thick, black air. I could now see my mistake in thinking that the looming structures were towers. I felt enlightened, but the revelation that standing before us were immense giants only served to exchange confusion with fear. I have seen towers just like these crowning the city walls at Montereggione in Italy. These terrifying giants had once been defeated by Jove and were still at the mercy of that god's thunderous power. Towers they weren't, but tower they did above the rim of that deathly silent pit.

Nimrod

I could already make out the face, shoulders, chest and most of the torso of one of them, and his arms were stuck fast to his sides. Nature had done well to stop making monsters such as these because by doing so, she deprived Mars of warriors who could easily have exterminated the human race. Although she happily produces large powerful species like elephants and whales, it is interesting to think about the fineness of her judgement. She didn't grant these animals the instrument of reason because when reason is added to an evil will or power, it is impossible for man to protect himself.

The giant's face seemed as long and large as the bronze statue of St Peter's pine cone in Rome, and the rest of his body was in the same proportion. Even though half his body was below the rim of the well, there was enough above that point that not even three tall Dutchmen standing on each other's shoulders could reach as high.

The brutish mouth began to howl the sweetest tune he was capable of. 'Raphèl maí amèche zabí almi.'

My guide said to him, 'You stupid idiot, you should stick to your horn rather than spurt gibberish if you need to vent your rage. You really are dumb. The horn is lying across your chest and it is tied to a rope which you'll find hanging around your neck if you're clever enough to look.'

Then Virgil turned to me and said, 'He is showing his true colours, that one. He is Nimrod, the first king of Babylon. He arrogantly believed he could build a tower that could reach Heaven. God was so offended that he split the single, universal language of the time, into countless different ones across the world causing a chaos in communication. Let's leave him alone. He doesn't even understand us. Our words are as much gibberish to him as his words are to us, so conversation is pointless.'

Ephialtes; Briareus

We turned left and went as far as you could shoot an arrow from a recurve bow until we came to a second giant who was more terrifying than the first. I don't know who had enslaved him, but heavy chains shackled his right arm behind his body and his other arm in front. The chains wrapped around his body five times from what I could see.

'This arrogant brute thought he could strong-arm supreme Jove, but look where he's ended up now,' said my guide. 'He is called Ephialtes and he threatened the gods by attempting to pile mountains on top of each other to climb up to Heaven. The arms he used to lift up mountains can lift no more.'

I knew of another chained giant called Briareus who had also been defeated by Jove. I asked Virgil where he was as I wanted to clap eyes on his immeasurable might. Virgil replied, 'You will see the giant Antaeus in a moment. He is unfettered as he was born after the war against the gods and we can communicate with him in an intelligent way. He is the one who will carry us down to the very depth of sin. Briareus who you are keen to see is much further round the rim and, while he is chained and tongue-tied like Ephialtes here, he looks even more ferocious.'

Hearing those words, Ephialtes shook more violently than an earthquake would need to shake a strong tower. He was supremely jealous that another could be deemed more ferocious than him and I was convinced I was about to die. In fact, I thought I might actually already be dead, except that I could still feel my fear, though that abated when, praise God, I saw his chains.

Antaeus

We ventured further and, at last, we came to Antaeus who towered the tallest above the rocky edge.

'You are the great giant who captured a thousand lions in the Tunisian valley where Scipio conquered Hannibal. Many people believe that, together with your fellow giants, you could have conquered Jove himself! We would be very grateful if you could perform a relatively small feat and carry us down below where the cold turns Cocytus to ice. We don't want to have to ask one of the rebel giants to help us. After all, this living man can bring good news of you to earth in exchange for your assistance, so please bend down and don't grunt or grimace.'

The giant brusquely stretched out his hands which had once gripped Hercules with all their might, and he picked up my dear guide. When Virgil felt himself lifted up, he called to me, 'Come closer so that I can catch hold of you.' He then clasped me tightly so that we were bundled together in that giant cup.

It was like looking up at the tower of Pisa when a cloud comes overhead. The cloud appears static and the tower seems to be leaning more and more. That was just how Antaeus looked when he started to stoop. At that moment, I really wanted to be in quite another place on quite another journey, but he set us gently down at the bottom of the abyss where Lucifer and Judas are encased. He didn't linger long and raised himself straight up again just as a capsized sailboat rights its mast to point back up at the sky.

CANTO 32

Traitors to Clients; Traitors to Charities

Stuck in Ice

The ninth circle of Hell is an icy lake called Cocytus which is divided into four increasingly evil parts. It houses the traitors. In the first, Sisyphus holds those traitors who betrayed people's trust or who breached a duty of care, such as doctors or teachers. The region is named after the first king of Corinth who was famous for trickery and used his wicked intelligence to cheat death itself. The second region, called Antenora, contains sinners who acted treacherously against charities or the very institutions which set out to help them and is named after a character in Homer's poem, the Iliad. The story developed in the middle ages when it was said that Antenora betrayed Troy to the Greeks and stole the Trojan Palladium, the icon that kept the city safe. All the traitors tend to want to reveal the name of every other soul but their own, as they don't want their infamy to be spread about on earth.

The lake of Cocytus

If I had sufficiently brutal and bitter words to describe this hell hole on which the other circles of Hell and the universe press down, I would need to squeeze the juice of my lexicon hard. But since I don't have the words, I am slightly anxious about the task I am compelled to complete. This is not a book of simple words for babies, nor is it for flippant folk. I need to do my journey justice. The sinners I witnessed here are an insidious rabble. They are condemned to the darkest, most evil place in all the world where words find the limits of their power.

Facing the rocky wall, we scrambled further into the evil well, going some way below the giant's feet. I was still looking up in wonderment at the height of the entire wall we had managed to navigate down when I heard a voice say, 'Be careful where you put your feet! Mind you don't tread on the heads of these weary wretched fellows.'

I turned and saw a huge expanse of ice spread out in front on me and beneath my feet. It had the appearance more of glass than of water. Even the continent of ice which forms the Antarctic with its freezing skies did not have ice as thick as this. Had the greatest mountain in the world tumbled onto that ice, it wouldn't have cracked.

Sisyphus; betrayers of clients

Looking at the souls buried here, I was reminded of frogs that poke their noses out of the water to soak up the late summer rays, sending their croaks reverberating around the surrounding fields. Yet these wretched souls stood trapped in ice up to their necks, frozen to the bone, their teeth chattering like storks. Their heads were bowed down in shame, grief poured from their eyes and their mouths uttered cold, mournful notes.

I looked all around and then, glancing down at my feet, I noticed a pair of souls huddled together so closely that you couldn't tell whose hair was whose. 'Tell me who you are,' I called, 'and why you are so bound together.'

They lifted their conjoined heads and looked up at me, but the tears which had been flowing from their eyes now froze over their cheeks and lips in the cold air, gluing them even tighter in a kiss. Clamped together like a barnacle to a boat, they were overcome with fury and butted their heads like rams in an attempt to break out of their enforced embrace.

Another soul, who had lost both ears from the cold and kept his head bent down, asked, 'What are you hoping to glean from us? If you want to know who those two are, they are brothers, Mark and Samuel, who lectured in history and physics at the same university. They were attracted to the same student and engaged in an inappropriate threesome. When they were found out by the university authorities, they fell out spectacularly and now they are forced to suffer in each other's embrace. There are plenty of worthy captives in this icy prison of Sisyphus. There is John Swanlond, a surgeon who claimed he could repair Agnes of Stratton's severely deformed hand. She trusted in his ability to cure her, and agreed to an operation, but the poor hand was even more mangled after the event. The one who is frozen solid right in front of me and blocking my view is Harold Shipman, the most perverted doctor you will ever hear about. He wrote fraudulent prescriptions for an addictive drug for himself and, over a number of years, he managed to kill two hundred and fifty of his trusting patients. They were mainly his older patients. He would lure himself into their homes on the pretext of caring for them, but he would administer lethal drugs to kill them and then he would change their wills to benefit himself. He truly believed he had the power of life or death over his patients but now he has come face to face with a power of a higher order than his own! Please don't ask any more questions, but briefly, I will come to be known as

Doctor Satan. I built a reputation as a good doctor in Paris, but I was hungry for money and power over my patients. I promised Jews wanting to escape from Nazi occupied France that my medicine could protect them from disease. In fact, it was poison. They received death a little earlier than they might have, and I received their worldly possessions. And look if it isn't Satan himself now holding the syringe in this ice-cold death trap!'

Antenora; betrayers of charities

I saw a thousand faces turned blue by the cold and I will shudder at the thought of the sight of it every time I pass an icy pond. I was shivering in the shadowy chill as we approached the centre where gravity bears the weight of the whole earth. I am not sure how it happened, but it would have been down to one of chance, fate or desire. As I went walking among the heads, I managed to kick one hard in the face.

Yéle

'Ow! What did you do that for? Why are you bothering me?' he railed. 'Have you come to make me pay even more for my betrayal of charitable donors?'

I asked Virgil to hold on for a moment as I was keen to find out who this arrogant soul was. I reproached the angry sinner. 'What right do you think you have to condemn other people?'

'Why don't you tell me who you are, marching through Antenora and kicking people about?' he replied. 'Even if you were alive, that kick was harder than I expected.'

'Well, actually, I am alive, and you could benefit greatly if you are interested in fame, as I could add your name to my recordings of this journey.'

He said, 'I am interested in quite the opposite. Get away from me and don't bother me anymore. Flattery and false promises get you nowhere in this ugly place!'

Riled, I quickly grabbed him by the hair at the back of his head and said, 'Tell me your name or I'll pull out your hair and make your brain freeze!'

'You may threaten to make me bald, but I am not going to tell you my name or show you my face even if you kick me a thousand times!'

I had already wrapped his locks around my hand and yanked out a clump of hair. He let out a loud yelp but kept his head pinned down, when another soul called out, 'What's got to you, Yéle? Is the clamour of chattering teeth not enough for you that you have to yelp out too? Put a lid on it for goodness sake.'

'Ah!' Virgil intervened. 'Yéle siphoned off a lot of charitable donations sent to give Haitians housing, water, sanitation and food after their earthquake killed two hundred and fifty thousand people and displaced five million people. The world will have seen how little money reached the people on the ground. All too often big charities subcontract aid work to foreign companies to revitalise the ravaged economy when they need to give more leadership to the local community. Local people are often mistreated and suffer sexual abuse by aid workers. There may also be financial leakage along the line. These donating countries need to track their funds right through the process. They need to be able to account for what is spent on labour and materials so that there is greater transparency. These charity frauds tragically divert desperately needed funds, they affect the morale of the decent charity workers and they erode public trust.'

'Right then, wretched traitor,' I said. 'I don't want to hear another word from you. I will be sure to tell everyone the truth about your shameful crime.'

'Get away,' he replied. 'Report whatever you want, but if you do actually leave this place, make sure you denounce the one whose tongue let slip my name. She is paying back for the benefit fraud she committed. Oh yes! She filled in fraudulent forms to apply for income support, housing benefit, disability living allowance, and social fund payments and then laundered the money through her daughter's bank account. You will be able to say: "I saw grasping, malicious Melissa, who cheated her government aid system, deep down where sinners are preserved in ice."'

Traitors to Family

Lying in Ice

The third region of Cocytus contains the traitors who betrayed members of their own family. This region is called Caina, named after Cain, who, in the Old Testament, was the first person to murder a member of his family.

King John tells the story of the fall of William de Braose and the imprisonment of William's wife, Maud, with their eldest son. While King John may feel remorse, neither he nor the political point scorer, William de Braose, deserve our pity. It is his wife and child who are the innocent victims of political feuding and civil strife. Human corruption and lack of loyalty to family, country or those who care for us represent the worst possible abuses of moral values. Their effect on innocent people is deeply shocking and unacceptable.

Caina; betrayers of family

We carried on to the next region of Cocytus, Caina, where the frost bitterly binds another set of souls, not upright this time, but flat on their backs. The very act of weeping staunches the flow of their tears. The first gush fills the socket's stoup to form a lump of ice like a crystal ball. Since their grief finds no outward trajectory, it turns back in on itself and pierces their core with increased pain.

I was frozen to the bone and had lost all feeling in my fingers and toes, but I felt a gentle gust of wind against my cheek and asked Virgil, 'I can feel wind in the air. How is that possible when everything is frozen solid down here?'

He answered, 'Be patient. You will see for yourself when we get closer.'

English kings: Henry II and his sons Richard I and John

My thoughts were distracted when I saw, lying in the ice, three souls frozen together in a single hole. They were packed so close that one head lay right on top of the other two. The uppermost head laid its teeth into one neck and used its hands to strangle the other. Hearing us approach, the ravenous soul lifted his head to break from his barbaric meal and, wiping his mouth on the hair of his gnawed victim, he called out to us, 'Help me please, cruel souls, who seem destined for the darkest circle in Hell. Remove the frosted crystal that covers my eyes so that I can vent the sorrow which wrings my heart before my tears turn to ice again.'

Unwilling to show mercy to sinners who had been cast so low, I asked, 'Why do you show your hatred for these two in such a brutish, savage way? Tell me who you are and, if you have a story to melt the world's hearts, then I will record it for those who live and breathe provided my tongue doesn't freeze before I leave this place. If you can meet this condition, you might find the ice thaws a little around your eyes.'

'I don't know who you are or why you are here, but I know I am obliged to respond to your request and will do anything to unfreeze myself from this numbing nihilism. I was King John of England and I am feasting on the head of my older brother, Richard, whilst strangling the neck of my father, King Henry. They say blood runs thicker than water, but I am not so sure. Anyway, this water has turned to solid ice so there's your proof. I was always jealous of Richard, for his successful exploits in France, and the fact that they called him "The Lionheart" irked me as I was portrayed as the evil one. In fact, Richard spent hardly any time in England, preferring to command territory in France and fight crusades over the Holy Land. I, at least, was concerned with matters at home, aiming to strengthen the English position in Ireland and Wales. My brother and I were both hungry for power and we ultimately conspired against our father to take the throne. Once Henry had died, Richard and I continued to feud. I attempted to seize Richard's kingdoms in France and, although forgiven for my betrayal, our feuding only ended with his unfortunate death in battle fighting against Philip II in France, when an arrow shot into his shoulder.

'The story I want to tell you is less well known but, if you can report it back to the world, people will see the effect that family and political feuding has on innocent victims. When I took the crown of England, William de Braose was my court favourite, but he was not free of treachery himself having lured Welsh leaders to a reconciliatory dinner only to have them murdered by his men. Still, I was generous to him, letting him keep his gains in Wales and giving him castles across the country. If the truth be known, and in Hell there is no hiding, he obliged me by murdering my nephew, Arthur, who Richard had named as his heir when he left for the crusades. I rewarded William richly for eradicating this obstacle to the throne. But then things turned sour. William's wife, Maud, and many nobles suspected me of murdering Arthur, and I needed to silence their wagging tongues. William also turned against me and sided with the Welsh in their rebellion against me. Now I seized William's estates in Sussex, Devon and Wales. I captured Maud and their eldest son, also called William, and I thrust them in the dungeon at Corfe Castle where they starved to death.

'Maud wrote a diary, found shortly after her ordeal, and it is only right that I share her words with the world.

'"William and I trusted John and we served him well, but we became victims of his capricious nature. He felt threatened by us and went after us. My husband William fled to France, disguised as a beggar and John captured my eldest son, William, and me. Hear just how cruel our death was. We found ourselves imprisoned in Corfe Castle inside the well-named "oubliette" where plenty of enemies of the king were banished, abandoned to their deaths. There was a small slit for a window in the thick stone wall and, through this, I could watch the moon and estimate how many months were passing. I had a terrible dream which revealed our impending future. King John appeared as master of the hunt, chasing a vixen and her cub through the woods and fields. He set trained and eager hounds on our scent and ran those little foxes to ground. The mother and baby fox flagged with exhaustion and their weakened flesh was stripped by those sharp fangs.

"When I awoke before dawn, I heard my son crying in his sleep, begging for bread. If you don't share my pain, then you are cold and cruel indeed, and if you aren't moved to tears at this point, then I wonder, do you ever cry? My son was awake by now and it was almost time for food to be brought to our door, but we both had a sense of foreboding about the meaning of our dreams. Then I heard the sound of nails being hammered into the door of the dungeon and I looked into my son's eyes without a word. I couldn't cry. I seemed turned to stone. But little William did shed tears and blubbed: "Mummy, what is it? What's the matter?" I still didn't weep, but neither did I answer his question all that day or that night. But when the sun rose the following day on that woeful prison, I saw my very own despair reflected in that innocent face and I clenched my hands in my mouth in misery. Thinking I was biting into my hands out of hunger, my child got to his feet and cried: "Mummy, I can't bear to see you hurt yourself. Please take my flesh for food. You brought me into this sorry life and made me flesh and bone, so take it now that you need it." I tried to control my grief to ease his worries. The whole of that day and the next were spent in silence. Cruel earth, why didn't you swallow us up then? On the fourth interminable day without food, sweet William wrapped his arms around my legs crying: "Mummy, help! Please, can't you help me?" There he died. Imagine the scene. I saw life leave my child. I was already blind by then and took to fumbling around his body calling out his name, even though he had been dead for two days. Finally, if grief almost killed me, it was starvation which finished me off."

'Frozen in time in this hellish lake, I am indeed filled with grief and you can see that I re-live Maud's starvation in eternal punishment.'

When he had finished speaking, he rolled his head like a madman and sank his teeth into his brother Richard's wretched skull, stripping the flesh back to the bone like a rabid dog.

Virgil was also moved by Maud's story and reasoned, 'Turning against William and imprisoning his wife and child were John's biggest mistakes. His ability to turn on his most trusted servants provoked mistrust among his barons and encouraged them to rebel against him. In turn, their rebellion led to the signing of the Magna Carta, forcing King John and future kings of England to observe the rule of common law and devolving power from the king's hands.'

Lucifer; Traitors to Country; the Journey through the Southern Hemisphere to the Edge of Earth

Encased in Ice

The final section of Cocytus is called Guidecca after Judas, who betrayed Christ. That betrayal foreshadows the evil and corruption which in later years become evident in the institution of the church. The same forces are at play in the secular world as Julius Caesar's cruel death showed. He was betrayed by Brutus and Cassius, displaying the destruction of good governance by evil forces. Caesar's death serves to remind us of the effects of political feuds and the greed for power throughout history and the world.

Dante scorns individuals who betray their political party, their government or their sovereign. Not standing true to one's allegiances is something that riles him and, as before, we are asked to accept that divine justice is not to be argued with.

Guidecca: betrayers of country

'*Vexilla regis* the regal banners of Hell are approaching; look ahead!' Virgil said. 'See if you can make out the King of Evil in this darkness.'

I could just about see the outline of a giant structure that looked like a windmill ahead of us, but it was like peering through thick fog or dusky shadows as night begins to fall. It is true that I could feel the wind blowing from that direction, and I tucked in behind my guide as there was nowhere else to shelter.

I am fearful of putting this in writing, but we had come to the final region of Cocytus where souls were utterly submerged in ice like carcasses encased in limpid glass. Some were lying, others were upright, some head up, some head down; others were arched back over themselves like gymnasts with their head close to their feet.

Virgil said, 'You won't be able to talk to these wretched sinners, as they are fully frozen and, anyway, you wouldn't be sure whether what they'd say would be true or treacherous.'

He pointed out Mathilde Carré, nicknamed "La Chatte", who served under the Polish secret service in occupied France during the Second World War. When her cover was blown, she switched to serve German military intelligence and betrayed one of her spy-ring with a kiss, echoing Judas. Blown again, and to save her skin, she agreed to serve the Polish secret service once more until she was incarcerated by the British.

He showed me President Nixon who spied on his political opposition in America to gain electoral advantage in a scandal that would come to be known as Watergate. Nixon was accused of treacherously covering up his party's involvement and, threatened with impeachment, he resigned. He is the only American president to do so in the history of the constitution.

We saw Harold "Kim" Philby who became a communist while at the University of Cambridge and later became a Soviet agent. He was recruited by British intelligence which the world will come to know as MI6. He betrayed the British by spilling the beans to the Soviets that there was a plan to send anti-communist troops into Albania, foiling their attack. His allegiance to the Soviets resulted in the betrayal of several western agents who lost their lives. Virgil showed me Mir Jafar, the Indian general who betrayed his troops to the British East India Company which were intent on monopolising trade in India following the fall of the Moghul Empire. His treachery landed him the title of Nawab, or ruler, in Bengal and he curried military favour with the East India Company, paying them large sums of money in return for assistance.

The final iced traitor whose name I will record here was Agent 006, Alec Trevelyan, who betrayed his MI6 employers to avenge the deaths of his Russian family. Trevelyan's parents had collaborated with the Nazis and, after what will be known as World War Two, they defected to Britain. However, the British authorities sent them back to the Soviet Union where many family members were executed by Stalin's death squads. His father, ashamed that he had escaped the death squads, ended up killing Trevelyan's mother and himself. Trevelyan was taken in and trained by MI6 but his loyalty was never with the British and he causes James Bond quite a bit of bother in the story people will come to know as GoldenEye. Traitors of government and country, the world over, can only be described as rotten right through, and I was glad not to indulge them by hearing their duplicitous words. What shame they have brought on themselves and their comrades!

Lucifer

By now we had drawn close enough to take in the creature who had once been able to boast of beauty. Virgil turned round to talk to me face on, and I gave him my full attention. 'You are about to meet the King of Hell. Take a deep breath and make sure you are ready for this.'

I froze with fear and felt quite faint but to try to describe the extent of my terror is pointless as words cannot do it justice. So please, dear reader, don't expect too much. I didn't die at that moment but neither did I remain alive. Imagine, if you can, what state I was in, given I had neither life nor death within me.

The emperor of this miserable realm was planted there in majesty, his chest protruding from the coffin of ice. One of his arms alone was larger than any giant – imagine the enormity! If he was once as fair as he is now foul, it is only right that his arrogant rebellion against his creator renders him the fount of all evil and sorrow in the world.

I couldn't believe it when I saw three faces on his head. The central one was crimson red; the other two were lodged either side, one on each shoulder; all three were joined in trinity. The face to the right was a yellowish white and the one to the left was a black as night. Each face commanded two mighty wings, as befitting such a horrific bird. These wings were fashioned not of feathers but of membrane like bats' wings, and the monster flapped and beat them so that three chill winds gushed forth to freeze that evil lake.

Wretched tears and blood oozed down over three chins from his six eyes. Each mouth devoured a sinner so that his teeth tortured three at a time. But for the sinner in the middle, the grinding teeth were nothing compared with the rasping claws which repeatedly stripped the skin from his back.

Judas, Brutus and Cassius

'The soul up there who suffers the greatest punishment', Virgil said, 'is Judas Iscariot. He has his head stuffed inside the central mouth and his legs are flailing about outside. Hanging from the blackest mouth is Brutus and you can watch him writhing although he betrays no sound. The third one is Cassius, and he has been stripped raw. But night is falling again, so we must leave this place. We have seen Hell in its entirety now.'

Dante and Virgil descend down Lucifer's body

Virgil invited me to wrap my arms around his neck and I clasped him close. Then, carefully judging the moment when the wings were stretched out widest, he leaped with me onto the shaggy monster and down we climbed, from shag to shag, between the matted fur and the crusts of ice.

When we had climbed half-way down that gargantuan body to the top of the thigh, my guide stopped and turned himself on his head as if he was about to climb straight back up again. It was no easy feat and, puffing and panting, he tugged and turned against those shaggy limbs until we seemed to be headed back to Hell.

'Hold on tight,' he said, gasping for breath. 'These are the stairs we now have to climb to put those evil ways behind us.'

At last, we crawled through an opening in the rock behind the beast's body and Virgil set me down to rest on a stone. He then stepped carefully away from the hairy monster and came towards me.

I lifted my gaze, expecting to see Lucifer's head as I had seen him before, but instead there were his mighty legs sticking up in front of me. I was discombobulated and confused at this point, but perhaps even an idiot can work out better than me where I was and what point in the earth's system I had crossed.

'Up you get now,' Virgil commanded. 'We've a long way to go. The path is rugged and the sun is already rising.'

Cast images of palatial ballrooms far from your minds. This was the furthest remove. We found ourselves in a small cave with a rough floor and little light.

Virgil explains the structure of the universe

As I straightened myself up to go on, I said, 'Master, before I leave this hateful abyss, please could you explain to me where the ice is now? And that monster there, how is it that he is now upside down? Also, how can we have arrived at morning already, when it was only just nightfall?'

'You think you are still on the far side of the universe where I caught hold of the hair of the evil worm that pierces the world's core. Well, we remained on the far side until I turned my body around. That was the point of the earth's centre of gravity and there we passed from the hemisphere of Earth with Jerusalem, the Holy Lord's place of crucifixion at its zenith, to the hemisphere of Sea. Here it is morning while there it is evening, and the King of Hell, who made a staircase for us out of his shaggy hair, stands just as he did before, with his top half in one hemisphere and his bottom half in the other. When Lucifer fell down from Heaven, earth fled in horror to the other side of the sea. Likewise, earthly paradise also fled to escape his clutches by pushing outwards from the earth's crust and creating the mountain which we are heading towards now.'

The climb to the surface of the earth

At the far end of the cave, you could hear the trickling sound of a little brook. This stream starts its journey in the foothills of earthly paradise and winds its way, hidden from view, down a gentle sloping course through the rock.

Virgil and I started towards the burbling brook and followed its invisible course back out to the bright world. On and up we climbed, not wanting to pause for rest. Virgil led the way and I followed on behind. On and on and up and up we went until, finally, I strained all my senses towards a round hole in the rock and witnessed the fruits of Heaven. We squeezed our bodies through the hole and rejoiced. And as soon as we were out on the other side, we could look once more upon the circling stars.

Cross-section of Earth

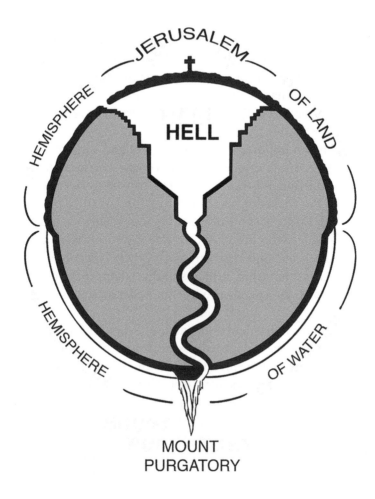

A Final Word and Acknowledgements

Uncomfortably, a part of every one of us will be contained within *Hell Unearthed* as it is impossible for humankind to be perfect. Indeed, there is not even perfection in evil. I have been keen to mirror Dante's ability to see both the good and the bad in many of the sinners selected to illustrate our complex nature. It is quite possible to strive for greatness on earth and to do the right thing by family, friends, political party or country, while also making bad choices which harm other people. Nothing is black and white and there are almost always two sides to every story.

If life isn't a human leveller, death certainly is. Dante had seen his world deteriorate into one of superficial greed for money and power, corruption of the church, and deception of loved ones. Perhaps having reached the middle of his life, he had become more aware of these evils. But nothing has really changed, has it? Our perception of sin has changed as society has developed and the modern world has evolved, but we see modern sinners falling prey to the same temptations and making the same errors in judgement as in ancient times.

Friendship plays an important part in our lives and Virgil performs this role perfectly for Dante. He is at once supportive and encouraging, chiding and challenging, but the undercurrent of love and constancy never wanes.

In amongst all the wickedness and suffering there is still a place for humour. We can laugh with Dante at some of the ridiculous scenes such as the wriggling legs of the authorities who are placed upside down in holes and the jocular demons who fight, argue and spar with each other. Life contains fear, anxiety and shock – but also friendship, love, inspiration, happiness, achievement and relief; with humour, we can deal with the bad parts. It is all here in *Hell Unearthed*.

Acknowledgements in particular to Natalino Sapegno, Dorothy L Sayers and Charles Singleton for their detailed research and commentary which have helped to shape as true an interpretation of Dante's intentions as possible.

It has been a delight to work with Rob Page, my illustrator. He has been thoughtful and responsive from the get-go and his creations have hit the spot perfectly. He has risen to the challenge of working with a totally new piece of literature and I hope that he has become an additional Dante fan.

Miles Bailey and his staff at the Choir Press have been unfailingly patient with my numerous questions and need for advice. Their service has been professional throughout, and the production process as well as the design of the book's cover have been seamless.

My deepest thanks go to my editor-in-chief, my husband, Simon, for his critical eye in helping me achieve as polished a piece of prose as possible. Despite a demanding job, he never snubbed the series of drafts I put under his nose and rigorously edited them in his valuable spare time.

Last, but by no means least, I should thank the writing contingent in my family, both past and present, whose various achievements in journalism, novels and autobiography have given me the inspiration and conviction to write.

Glossary

Here you will find characters by first name and by canto. Further information, if you want to read deeper, is provided in italics.

Aaron Burr (Canto 12). American politician and lawyer. 3rd Vice President of the US, serving under the Republican Thomas Jefferson from 1801-1805.

Alexander Hamilton was a Federalist who believed in a strong, central government. He was Secretary of the Treasury under the first President, George Washington. Hamilton was opposed to Burr and made his views public. This persistent animosity thwarted Burr's political ambitions and led to Burr challenging Hamilton to a duel in 1804. He fatally wounded Hamilton and is punished in Hell Unearthed *for grievous bodily harm. Hamilton died from his wounds the following day.*

Achilles (Canto 14). Greek warrior and hero of Homer's *Iliad.* Homer relates how Achilles was killed in the siege of Troy.

Dante adopted the later story that Achilles fell in love with Polyxena, the daughter of King Priam of Troy, and he was promised her hand in marriage on condition that he side with the Trojans. Achilles ventured unarmed into a Trojan temple and, in an act of deception by the Trojans, was assassinated by Paris, Priam's son.

Adolf Hitler (Canto 14). German dictator 1933-1945 and leader of the Nazi Party.

His rise to power coincided with economic recovery and falling unemployment which, together with terror unleashed on the public by the police, solidified his regime. His attack on Poland marked the start of the Second World War. He started by conquering western and central Europe before turning his attention to Russia in the East. Alongside his international military aggression, and elimination of any political opponent, he was also responsible for the mass genocide of Jewish people, killing millions of Jews in the course of the Second World War.

Al Capone (Canto 26). American gangster crime boss during the prohibition era in the 1920s and 1930s.

He ran prostitution, gambling and bootlegging businesses, selling alcohol at a time when booze was banned. At twenty-one, he got into a tussle and had his left cheek slashed which led to the nickname "Scarface". In 1931, he was charged with tax evasion and conspiracy to violate prohibition law. He was sentenced to prison, including five years at Alcatraz.

Antaeus (Canto 31). Son of Neptune and Tellus, gods of sea and earth respectively.

A giant who was invincible as long as he was in touch with his mother, Earth. Hercules managed to overcome him by lifting him up in the air and squeezing him to death. Antaeus is left unchained in Hell because he was not one of the giants who fought against the gods. Unlike Nimrod, his speech is comprehensible. He is said to have lived in the desert and fed on lions.

Arsène Lupin (Canto 21). Fictional gentleman thief and master of disguise, moonlighting as a detective. He was a character in novels by Maurice Leblanc in 1905 in response to the popularity of Arthur Conan Doyle's *Sherlock Holmes* stories which were popular in Europe and America.

The concept of the gentleman thief was popular in French literary culture at the time, following a sensational real-life case of a gentleman burglar who had committed a hundred robberies before being brought to trial. In the books, Arsène Lupin uses various disguises such as chauffeur, bookmaker, detective, Spanish bullfighter, or decrepit old man. When his character became popularised on stage, he was depicted as a suave man wearing a tuxedo with white gloves, a monocle, a top hat and carrying a cane.

Artemisia Gentileschi (Canto 13). Successful 17th century female Italian baroque painter who painted in the style of Caravaggio.

She was tutored in painting by her father, assisting him with his own works of art. She was raped by one of her father's painting friends, Tasso, when she was 17. When he failed to fulfil his promise to marry her, Artemisia's father brought him to trial and Artemisia had to give evidence under torture. She was the first woman to join Florence's Academy of Design in 1616.

Beaumont children (Canto 22). Three children, aged 9, 7 and 4 were abducted from Glenelg beach in Adelaide, Australia on Australia Day in 1966. They had gone on an outing by bus without their parents and their bodies have never been located. Arthur Stanley Brown was later arrested for a separate abduction of two schoolgirls but he escaped conviction. A retrial was scheduled but he was deemed unfit to stand trial following a diagnosis of Alzheimer's. He died in 2002. It is thought that his profile fits a further abduction of two girls from the Adelaide Oval as well as the Beaumont children abduction.

Beatrice (Canto 1). Her role in Hell is to lead Dante through Purgatory into Paradise to reach God and salvation. She beseeches Virgil to rescue Dante from his bewilderment and terror in the dark woods.

She was born in 1266 and lived in Florence in Dante's time. She was a member of the Portinari family and Dante tells us in his work La Vita Nuova – The New Life, *that he fell in love with her when they were aged 8 and 9 respectively having met at a May Day party at her father's house in Florence. He then idolised her in his writing and she became a muse or inspiration for him. She died when she was only 24 and Dante gives her blessed status through his writing. In the* Divine Comedy *she is both a saint and a beautiful woman. She represents happiness, grace and virtue and acts as man's guide to redemption.*

Bernie Madoff (Canto 27). Worked in investment management on Wall Street and made his name in pioneering electronic trading. He was an apparently successful hedge fund manager who claimed he was investing in blue chip stocks and achieving consistent double digit returns at a time when other funds were trailing the market.

He built a reputation of exclusivity around his funds and many clients were charities, so no one questioned the operation for years. In reality he was putting investors' money in a bank account and paying out returns from new investments received. Then a whistle-blower contacted the SEC, challenging the ability to make returns on that scale at a time when the market started to fall. He also claimed that Bernie was taking commissions higher than the standard rate and that he was taking out large bank loans to support the business. A run of client redemptions crippled the business, the truth came out and Bernie received a life sentence for fraud. He died in 2021 and is therefore a recent entrant to Hell Unearthed.

Black Mamba (Canto 12). Protagonist in Quentin Tarantino's 2003 film, *Kill Bill*. Black Mamba was Beatrix Kiddo's code name when she worked for the Deadly Viper Assassination Squad under her ex-lover, Bill. She is a formidable, ruthless warrior trained in martial arts.

Bill is jealous that Kiddo is starting a new life and getting married to someone else. He gate-crashes the wedding rehearsal and shoots everyone including Kiddo, who is left in a coma for four years. When she recovers, she sets about taking revenge on Bill and her fellow Vipers.

Boniface VIII, Pope (Canto 3). Pope 1294-1303. Dante's most hated character. Boniface deceived his predecessor, Celestine, to renounce the papacy thereby getting himself elected. He believed that what belonged to the church was his own. He also pulled favours for his family.

Pope Nicholas III spills the beans that Boniface will go to Hell even though Boniface is still alive at the time the story is set in 1300.

Dante vents his anger at the damage done to the church as popes like Boniface wanted power that extended beyond the spiritual realm of the church and they interfered with the affairs of government which were supposed to be the preserve of temporal powers such as a king or a political party. Dante is also aggrieved because it was Boniface who ordered his exile from Florence.

Bonnie and Clyde (Canto 20). American criminal couple who travelled around America undertaking a number of bank and store robberies during the Great Depression of the 1930s.

Their robberies made the newspaper headlines, and the pair milked media attention by circulating staged photographs of themselves playing around with stolen cars and guns. The public loved reading about the couple's open defiance of the law. After a prolonged manhunt to bring them to justice, they were shot to death by officers in an ambush in Louisiana in 1934.

Briareus (Canto 31). Son of the goddess, Tellus, the Earth. A giant who fought against the Olympians.

Brutus (Canto 34). A devoted supporter of the Roman Republic which was governed by elected officials. Even though Pompey had killed his father, Brutus sided with him in the civil war. When Pompey was later defeated, the anti-republican Roman dictator, Julius Caesar, pardoned him and gave him favours and positions of influence. However, he was persuaded by Cassius to murder Caesar for the good of the Republic.

Cacus (Canto 21). Depicted as a centaur, he was a son of Vulcan and lived in a cave on the Aventine Hill near Rome. He stole the oxen belonging to Geryon, which Hercules was bringing from Spain as one of his twelve labours.

Hercules had killed Geryon and had brought the oxen to Mount Aventine near Cacus's cave. Cacus led the stolen oxen by their tails making them walk backwards so that their hoofprints looked like they were leaving the cave, not entering it. However, the plan was foiled when Hercules heard the oxen bellowing and, drawn to the cave, he killed Cacus and recovered the oxen.

Calypso (Canto 13). A sea nymph who features in Homer's epic poem, the *Odyssey*. She saves Ulysses (Odysseus in the Greek) from his shipwreck when he washes onto the shore of her island, Ogygia. She holds him captive there for seven years and, using her unchecked feminine power, she repeatedly rapes him.

Her mortal victim weeps every day, longing for home. He eventually escapes when the Greek goddess, Athena, intervenes on his behalf, sending the messenger, Hermes, to tell Calypso to release him.

Cassius (Canto 34). Complicit with Brutus in the murder of the Roman dictator, Julius Caesar, on 15th March 44 BC. Like Brutus, he supported the Republic, but after Pompey's defeat, Cassius surrendered to Caesar. Cassius was pardoned and was promised positions of influence. However, he always saw Caesar as his enemy and convinced Brutus to join him in murdering the dictator.

Catherine the Great (Canto 18). Empress of Russia from 1762 until 1796 and the country's longest reigning female leader.

She was dedicated to Russia's participation in pan-European politics and culture and added Crimea and much of Poland to the Russian Empire. Her husband and second cousin, Peter III, was neurotic, obstinate and possibly impotent, and she had a string of lovers during their marriage. There is some debate as to whether any of her children, even the heir apparent, Paul, were fathered by Peter although this is convincingly contested. Catherine was ambitious and saw, in her husband's weakness, an opportunity to take over the government of Russia herself. She may have spread rumours about Paul's bloodline just to get him out of the way, freeing the way for her to become Empress. As Peter's popularity declined, she drew the military to her side and staged a coup, forcing Peter to abdicate the throne and paving the way for her to take his place.

Celestine V, Pope (Canto 3). Celestine became pope in 1294 and five months later he abdicated because he didn't feel up to the job. His abdication paved the way for Boniface VIII to become pope in his place.

Cerberus (Canto 6). Three-headed hound whose role is to guard the gates of Hell and preside over the souls of the greedy. He rages uncontrollably and devours the souls he is meant to guard.

Charles Lindbergh Junior (Canto 22). 20-month-old baby and son of aviator Charles Lindbergh. The baby was kidnapped from the family home in New Jersey in 1932 and a $50,000 ransom was demanded for his release. This was later increased to $70,000.

In a series of fraught communications between family intermediaries and the kidnapper, the kidnapper claimed that the baby was in good care, but two months later, the baby's body was discovered less than five miles from the family home. The baby was found to have died shortly after the kidnapping from a blow to the head. After a lengthy investigation involving the public and intelligence from the criminal underworld, a German immigrant carpenter, Bruno Hauptman, was charged with extortion and murder and was executed by electric chair in 1936.

Charles Ponzi (Canto 27). Italian immigrant living in Boston, America, in the 1920s. He made $15 million in eight months by persuading thousands of Bostonians that he could give them unbeatable returns on their investments. By attracting a stream of investors to his fraudulent scheme, he used the cash provided by new investors to pay the returns on older clients' investments.

Ponzi's name has now been given to all such schemes, also known as pyramid schemes. Ponzi arrived in America with apparently only $2.50 in his pocket having lost the remainder of his savings in games of cards on the ship that brought him over from Italy. Like many other young Italian men at the time, Ponzi was coming to America to seek *his fortune and enrich his family back home. He found menial work in New York and Florida before being taken on as a clerk in Boston. He married and took over his father-in-law's grocery business but with little success.*

His actual investment scheme was founded on the idea of pre-paid postal reply coupons where he could arbitrage currencies between the country where the coupons were bought and the US where the currency was usually stronger. While returns could feasibly make 10% in this way, Ponzi lied about the scale of his operation, and his promise of 50% or 100% returns was totally unfounded. Still, he persuaded clients ranging from other Italian working-class immigrants to policemen and politicians to invest. Soon he owned a mansion, fine cars and luxury jewellery, and had large corporate investments. Eventually, postal and legal authorities as well as local newspapers launched an investigation into Ponzi's affairs and discovered he was insolvent. Investments immediately dried up and the operation fell apart. The mutual saving bank holding the Ponzi deposits and financing the loans for repayments crashed as investors rushed to cash in their cheques. Ponzi was imprisoned for fraud.

Charon (Canto 3). Hell's ferryman and a character from classical literature.

Dante implicitly praises Virgil's writing, and all of classical literature, by borrowing features from the ancient writers to describe Charon. Virgil describes Charon in the Aeneid *as a terrifying guardian of the waters with an unkempt white beard and fiery eyes and a filthy old cloak hanging from his shoulders. Charon refuses Dante passage across the river just as he did with Aeneas in Virgil's* Aeneid *because they are both living souls in the underworld and, as such, it is not their place to be travelling through Hell. Charon tells Dante that he needs a lighter craft to carry him to salvation implying that he won't go to Hell after his death.*

Chiron (Canto 14). Leader of the centaurs, who are guardians of the violent. The centaurs are half-man, half-horse. In classical literature, the centaurs are angry and love to fight and pillage.

Chiron was a son of Saturn and taught Achilles and Hercules how to fight. He is authoritative and wise.

Ciacco (Canto 6). A Florentine famous for his greed and nicknamed "Ciacco" meaning "pig". Ciacco is also an abbreviation of the name Giacomo which was his full name, so you could say the name and the person were one and the same.

Clement V (Canto 30). Pope 1305-1314. He was regarded as totally selfish. It was said that Clement had bought his way to be pope by bribing King Philip the Fair of France with all of the church's income tax for five years.

Cleopatra (Canto 5). Queen of Egypt 51-30 BC, mistress of Caesar and then Mark Antony. She was famous for her beauty and seductive ways. She committed suicide in order to avoid being taken prisoner by Octavian, the future Emperor Augustus, who conquered Egypt, annexing it to Rome.

David Bowie (Canto 4). English rock star known as a musical chameleon for his ever-changing appearance and sound. He was born in Brixton as David Jones. His first hit was *Space Oddity* in 1969, which coincided with the Apollo 11 moon landing. In addition to being an influential musician, he was also a successful actor. He died of cancer in 2016.

Dennis Nilsen (Canto 15). Scottish serial killer who murdered at least twelve boys between 1978 and 1983 in his home in London. He was sentenced to life in prison and died in 2018.

> *He trained as a chef in the army, worked as a junior constable, a security guard and a placement officer for a Jobcentre. He was described by colleagues as quiet and conscientious. The majority of his victims were homeless or gay, but others were heterosexual. They were loners or vulnerable boys and he lured them to his home with the promise of alcohol or shelter. He plied them with drink and then strangled and drowned them before cutting up their bodies and disposing of them. The murders were first discovered by Dyno-Rod who had been called out by both Nilsen and neighbouring tenants to fix a blocked drain. Flesh and bones were found inside the pipework.*

Diana, Princess of Wales (Canto 5). First wife of Charles, Prince of Wales, when heir to the British throne, and mother to Princes William and Harry. It was an unhappy marriage which culminated in divorce in August 1986. Diana died in a tragic car accident in Paris only one year later in August 1987. Her boyfriend, Dodi Fayed, and Henri Paul, who was driving the car, also died. Her bodyguard, Trevor Rees-Jones, survived the crash.

Diego Maradona (Canto 19). Argentine footballer and joint winner of the FIFA player of the 20th century award alongside the Brazilian, Pelé.

> *He was highly skilled in passing, dribbling and striking and was well known for his small stature. He played in four World Cups and captained Argentina in the 1986 World Cup in Mexico, leading his team to victory over West Germany in the final. He received the Golden Ball as the tournament's best player. He was banned from football in 1991 and 1994 for drug abuse. He coached the national Argentinian team in the 2010 World Cup in South Africa and spent his latter career coaching and managing various club sides.*

Diomedes (Canto 19). King of Argos and one of the Greek heroes who besieged Troy.

Doctor Satan (Canto 32). Nickname given to Marcel Petiot. Petiot joined the army and then turned to medicine in 1921, practising in Villeneuve-sur-Yonne, France. Two of his patients were murdered but he avoided any charge. With the arrival of the Second World War, he planned to enrich himself by pretending to help Jews wishing to escape Nazi-occupied France. He injected them with poison telling them it was medicine to protect them against disease. After he watched them die, he stole their money and valuables and placed their bodies in the basement of his house. After the liberation of Paris in 1944, he was arrested, and thirty corpses were found under the floorboards. He admitted to killing sixty people and was sentenced to the guillotine in 1946.

Ebenezer Scrooge (Canto 7). Protagonist of *A Christmas Carol*, written by Charles Dickens in 1843. Scrooge is a cold-hearted miser who despises Christmas because giving is the antithesis of his being.

Elizabeth Taylor (Canto 18). Academy award-winning British-American actress. She married eight times and had numerous affairs during her marriages. The most scandalous affair was with Richard Burton, as they worked together on films and were both married when they started their affair. It was a tumultuous relationship with lavish gifts and exotic holidays, but they clashed and fought, and both succumbed to alcoholism. They married each other twice, 1964-1974 and 1975-1976.

Elvis Presley (Canto 6). One of the greatest names in rock and roll from the 1950s to the 1970s. Addicted to painkillers, he died of heart failure in 1977 at the age of 42.

Ephialtes (Canto 31). Son of Neptune, god of the sea. A giant who fought against the gods and threatened to pile Mount Pelion on top of Mount Ossa which would in turn be stacked on top of Mount Olympus in order to reach Heaven. He was slain by the Olympian god, Apollo.

Farinata (Canto 15). Leader of the Ghibelline party from 1239, he played an important part in politics in Florence and contributed to the banishment of the Guelphs in 1248.

When the Guelphs returned to Florence and the struggle against the Ghibelline party started up again, he was banished from the city with his Ghibelline tribe in 1258. He took refuge in Siena where, with the help of King Manfred, he strengthened the Ghibelline troops. They went on to win the battle of Montaperti in 1260, taking back control of the Tuscan district. Following Farinata's death in 1264, the Guelphs took control of Florence and, in revenge against Farinata's family (the Uberti), they exiled members of the family and razed their palaces to the ground. Farinata was posthumously condemned for Heresy, which, in medieval times, was a crime against the state as well as against the church.

Although he was an adversary of Dante's Guelph party, Dante is sympathetic to the strength and courage Farinata showed in leading his party and fighting for the political cause and the country he believed in. In Hell Unearthed, Dante is respectful towards this great man at their meeting but, nonetheless, Farinata is placed amongst the violent souls for the lives he killed in battle. Farinata's character conveys the contrast between greatness achieved temporally on earth, and divine judgement which is eternal.

Farmer B (Canto 27). Fictionalised character who planted jars of baby food, which he had laced with metal shards, on supermarket shelves. He demanded payment from the stores in return for telling them which jars were affected. The stores were forced to recall their lines of baby food but not before families had been dangerously exposed to the contaminated food. The perpetrator claimed he was part of a cohort of farmers who were protesting at the low retail price of milk which was eroding their profits.

FWA (Canto 24). Fictionalised character who procured money through deception, impersonation and forgery. He defrauded banks of millions of pounds by forging bank cheques and is punished with the counterfeiters in the 8th circle of *Hell Unearthed*.

George Best (Canto 6). Northern Irish professional footballer who played as a winger. He spent much of his career playing for Manchester United and is remembered for his skilful ability to dribble the ball past the opposition. He died in 2005 at the age of 59 from a long-standing addiction to alcohol and finds himself punished for excessive consumption in the 3rd circle of *Hell Unearthed*.

In 1966 at the age of 19, Best played for Manchester United in the European Cup against the Portuguese club, Benfica, in Lisbon. He scored two goals in the opening minutes and led his team to a 5-1 victory in the Portuguese side's first defeat at home since they'd started playing in Europe.

Geri del Bello (Canto 10). Cousin of Dante's father. Dante's sons relate that Geri was killed by one of the Sachetti family. There was plenty of antipathy between the Sachetti and Alighieri families resulting in a number of vengeful deaths. Peace between the two families was reached only in 1342 thanks to the Duke of Athens, who organised an official act of reconciliation.

In Dante's time, vengeful killing of rival family members was seen as an honourable duty and a given right. Dante took the view, and indeed over time laws and statutes developed in the same way, that these private killings were inexcusable in the interests of peace and the Christian ethos of living in harmony with one's neighbours.

Geryon (Canto 16). Colourful beast representing fraud with a lovely man's face and the body of a serpent with a poisonous forked tail. Geryon takes Dante and Virgil down from the 7th to the 8th circle of Hell, Evil Pits, where souls have abused their gift of intelligence to harm others through deceit.

In classical mythology, Geryon was a supremely cruel king from the Balearics. He was killed by Hercules in one of his twelve labours. Ancient poets depicted Geryon with a three-part body. Geryon would lure his guests in with sweet words and courtesy and, having coaxed them to sleep, he would kill them. Dante's depiction of the beast may have been influenced by sculptures on pulpits and bas-reliefs in Romanesque churches which were often decorated with fantastical creatures.

Han van Meegeren (Canto 24). A Dutch painter and portraitist. Considered one of the most ingenious art forgers of the 20th century.

He lived and worked in relative obscurity and, offended that his art was criticised for its lack of originality, he decided to take revenge by making forgeries in the style of the Dutch Old Masters. He planned to release them to the art world and, if accepted and admired, he would then reveal them as hoaxes. His most famous forgery was Supper at Emmaus, *depicting Christ breaking bread with two of his disciples after his resurrection from the dead. It was forged in the style of 17th century Vermeer and in 1937 it was received as a new find with great excitement in the art world. He had duped the experts so thoroughly that he decided to keep them ignorant of the true workmanship and produced several more forgeries. He was charged with treason when he was found to have sold a Vermeer to the Nazis but, in his defence, he admitted it had been a fake. Instead of treason, he was convicted of obtaining money by deception.*

Harold Shipman (Canto 32). English doctor found guilty of murdering fifteen elderly patients in his care but suspected of having killed up to two hundred and fifty between 1971 and 2000.

He was brought up in a working-class family in Manchester. His mother had lung cancer and would inject herself with morphine to manage the pain. It is thought that he was motivated by his mother's illness to go into medicine. He became a doctor but was found out to have written fraudulent prescriptions for an addictive drug for himself and was forced out of the practice. He established himself at another practice in Hyde and earned trust and respect in the community. He would visit patients in their homes, inject them with a lethal dose of painkiller and certify the death as natural.

Harpagon (Canto 7). Central character in Molière's *L'Avare* or The Miser, a play first performed in Paris in 1668. Harpagon is a bourgeois sexagenarian who is obsessed with the wealth he has amassed. At the same time, he is exaggeratedly penny-pinching to the extent that he refuses to replace the worn-out clothes of his overworked servants. Money is more important than love or family and he is deserving of his place amongst the money-grubbers in the 4th circle of *Hell Unearthed*.

Horatio Nelson (Canto 18). 1758-1805; British naval commander. He won important victories against Napoleonic France in the battle of the Nile, blowing Napoleon's ambitions of conquering the East; and in the battle of Trafalgar, destroying French and Spanish fleets and securing protection for the British Isles from invasion by sea for the next hundred years. He had a love affair with Emma, Lady Hamilton, while both were still married. He lost his life on HMS Victory at the Battle of Trafalgar having been shot by a French sniper.

Iceberg Slim (Canto 25). American pimp who became a famous author with the publication of his memoir about pimping in 1967. Iceberg Slim operated a prostitution business managing both white and black women in Chicago from the 1930s through to the 1950s. Prostitution was a symptom of poverty which was endemic across the board in the Great Depression of the 1930s. However, inequality between white and black Americans meant that black Americans continued to be deeply entrenched in poverty for a whole generation. Pimping effectively fed off that poverty. Iceberg Slim referred to his pimping days, describing himself as a "counter-revolutionary" as he exploited black Americans when, particularly as one of their community, he should have been fighting for their civil rights.

It is believed that he was driven to pimping by a hatred of women stemming from a hatred of his mother. He blamed her for having allowed a babysitter to sexually abuse him as a child and for having taken him away from his stepfather whom he'd loved. In

*the book, he says that he recognised that his hatred was misplaced, and he was able to
put pimping behind him because of his mother's unconditional love for him.*

*He claimed the book was a vehicle for purging himself of his evil past and he did not
set out to glamourise pimping, but rather, to expose the brutal reality of the industry at
a time when black Americans, who had been segregated to live in ghettoes, began to
revolt against the authorities in defiance at civil rights abuses. Iceberg Slim is said to
have been an inspiration for gangsta rap.*

Jacopo Rusticucci (Canto 15). Florentine Guelph of humble origins but a distinguished
statesman. He worked on political and diplomatic affairs with his close neighbour,
Tegghiaio Aldobrandi.

Jay Gatsby (Canto 7). Jay Gatsby is the protagonist in F. Scott Fitzgerald's 1925 novel *The
Great Gatsby*. The story is set in the Jazz Age on Long Island, America. Gatsby has a house
in West Egg, a middle-class area for the nouveau riche. He lays on a series of lavish parties
apparently in an attempt to woo an old flame, Daisy, who lives in East Egg, home to the
established upper class. He suffers with the wasteful sinners for his reckless spending.

Jimmy Savile (Canto 23). English DJ, TV and radio host of shows such as *Top of the Pops*
and *Jim'll Fix It*. He raised over £40 million for various charities and was knighted in 1990.
He died in 2011 and one year later, shocking evidence emerged that, over a fifty-year
period, he had sexually abused hundreds of vulnerable children and adults of both sexes
aged between 5 and 75. Indecent acts and rape occurred mainly at NHS hospitals which he
visited for fundraising and at the BBC where he worked.

John Paul Getty III (Canto 22). Grandson of oil tycoon, J. Paul Getty who was once the
richest person in the world but also renowned for being a cheapskate. Following his
parents' divorce in 1964, John Paul Getty III moved to Rome as a young teenager with his
father. His stepmother died of a heroin overdose in 1971 and, although his father returned
to England, he remained in Rome by himself. In 1973, aged 16, John Paul Getty III was
kidnapped by the 'Ndrangheta, a mafia organisation based in Calabria. A ransom note was
sent to his mother demanding $17 million.

*The family doubted the verity of the kidnapping as not only was John Paul errant and
rebellious, but he had previously joked that he would fake his own kidnapping in order
to extract money from his rich grandfather. His rich and penny-pinching grandfather
refused to pay the ransom and the child's kidnappers cut off an ear and a lock of hair,
sending them in the post to a newspaper in Rome as proof of their demands. They also
sent pictures of John Paul with his ear cut off. After five months, he was eventually
released.*

John Swanlond (Canto 32). London surgeon who was charged with breach of contract in 1374 for having carried out a bungled operation on the hand of his patient, Agnes of Stratton. Her hand had been mangled in an accident and the surgeon had guaranteed to cure her hand in return for reasonable payment. Unfortunately, the hand ended up more deformed than before the operation and this case became the precursor for medical malpractice litigation in common law.

Judas Iscariot (Canto 34). One of Jesus' disciples and the one who betrayed him to the Romans in exchange for thirty pieces of silver leading to Jesus' arrest and crucifixion.

King John (Canto 33). King of England from 1199 until 1216. Fourth adult surviving son of Henry II and Eleanor of Aquitaine. He succeeded his brother, Richard I, who was nicknamed Richard the Lionheart.

John's family life was fraught with disputes over power and land. Henry favoured his youngest son, John, and the three older brothers disputed Henry's intention to split his lands across France and Britain equally between them. Upon the death of the eldest son, Henry, Richard became heir, but the other sons, including John, continued to oppose their father up until his death in 1189.

While King Richard was away fighting in the Third Crusade, John tried to win over the people of London by promising them self-rule if they recognised him as heir apparent.

King Richard had some success in the Holy Land but Jerusalem evaded him. On his return from the crusades, Richard was captured by Leopold V, Duke of Austria. Leopold had suspected Richard of murdering his cousin, the King of Jerusalem, as part of a strategy to control the region. Richard was handed over to Leopold's ally, Henry VI, the Holy Roman Emperor, who demanded a ransom for his release.

Jealousies were at play as John sided with England and the Angevin Empire's enemy, Philip II of France, and tried to keep Richard imprisoned and away from England. Henry II's wife, Eleanor, paid the ransom by pawning the crown jewels. John's route to the throne was clear in that his older brother, Geoffrey, had died during Richard's reign. However, it was threatened by Geoffrey's son, Arthur, whose claim to the throne should have come ahead of John's. Arthur's death remains a mystery, but suspicion falls on John who had the biggest motive to eliminate him.

Lily Bart (Canto 7). Protagonist in Edith Wharton's 1905 novel, *The House of Mirth*. Lily is desperate to cling onto her status amongst high society in New York at the end of the 19th century. She spends what little money she has on luxurious dresses and gambling, and when her debts mount up, she entrusts her savings to a married man for investment. Her reputation is spoiled by her immoral associations, and vicious gossip destroys friendships and family ties. Cast out from society, she declines into penury and depression.

Lucifer (Canto 34). He was the most beautiful of God's angels, but he led the rebellion against God and was sent to Hell where he reigns as king. He is transformed from the most beautiful to the ugliest of God's creations.

Madame Claude (Canto 25). Owner of an elite French brothel in 1960s Paris, recruiting call girls for high-end dignitaries and civil servants.

She invented the term "call girl" by introducing a telephone-only booking system. She trained her girls to be entertaining company for her clients both in and out of the bedroom. She started her business from her flat on the Rue de Marignan in the 8th arrondissement in Paris, centrally located off the Champs-Elysées. From there she could recruit actresses, models, "it-girls" and, in return, she gave them money, discretion and protection. She also gave them a rags-to-riches makeover. They were dressed in Dior and Chanel outfits and she paired them off with plastic surgeons, princes and diplomats. As the business took off, she relocated to the 16th arrondissement above a branch of Rothschild bank. Her recruits had to be at least 175cm tall and she moulded her "Claudettes", as she called them, with plastic surgery if she deemed it necessary. She taught them about deportment and controlled everything about their appearance. She had them tutored in arts, politics and philosophy and their sexual skills had to pass muster so that they became cultured, beautiful, sexy companions. The French government eventually charged her with tax evasion and illegal pimping, and she was imprisoned.

Mary Butterworth (Canto 24). An American counterfeiter of bank notes. She started operations in 1716 in Massachusetts which was then a British colony. She used starched cotton cloths to produce counterfeit bank notes rather than the more commonly used copper plates.

Counterfeiting was damaging the economy and colonial authorities clamped down on the practice with convictions resulting in ears being cropped, whipping, fines or imprisonment. Although Mary Butterworth was brought to trial, there was not enough evidence to convict her and she gave up the practice at that point.

Maximus the Gladiator (Canto 12). Fictionalised character from Ridley Scott's film *Gladiator*, released in 2000, and played by Russell Crowe. Maximus was a high-ranking Roman general fighting under the Roman Emperor Marcus Aurelius and was highly favoured by the emperor. He had a strong sense of duty and loyalty.

Aurelius's son, Commodus, was jealous that the title of Emperor may be taken from him by Maximus. He set out to kill his father and then attempted to kill Maximus, who escaped. On the run, Maximus was sold to an old gladiator and, proving himself to be an excellent swordsman, he was rewarded with public applause when faced with the best gladiators in the Colosseum in Rome.

Medusa (Canto 9). According to Greek literature, Medusa was a Gorgon, a hideous winged monster with a human face, claws, and snakes for hair.

Medusa was the only mortal Gorgon. When she was a girl, she offended the goddess Athene, who turned her into a Gorgon with such an ugly face that anyone who looked into it turned to stone. She was finally killed by Perseus who managed to avoid her gaze and slay her by looking not directly at her but at her reflection in a shield.

Minos (Canto 5). King of Crete and Hell's judge. It is his job to hear the souls' confessions and hand out their punishment.

Minotaur (Canto 12). Guardian of the landslide at the 7th circle. Half-man, half-bull, the Minotaur was conceived of Pasiphaë, the wife of King Minos of Crete, and a beautiful bull. Daedulus disguised Pasiphaë as a cow so that the bull would reciprocate her advances. Dante depicted the Minotaur with the body of a bull and the head of a man which is the opposite to classical literature.

King Minos kept the Minotaur in the labyrinth at Knossos and, when he won a war against Athens, he demanded an annual supply of seven youths and seven maidens to be fed to the Minotaur. The Minotaur was killed by Theseus, son of the King of Athens, who had been sent to Crete to free his country from further human sacrifices by getting rid of the beast. Theseus fell in love with Ariadne, the daughter of Minos and Pasiphaë, who left a trail of thread to help him find his way out of the labyrinth.

Myra Hindley (Canto 15). Accomplice of Ian Brady in the Moors Murders in which five children, aged between 10 and 17, were sexually tortured and killed between 1963 and 1965 around Manchester.

Hindley's father was an alcoholic who beat his wife and taught his daughter to stand up for herself by fighting back against bullies. She was obsessed with dead and mangled bodies of animals and felt no empathy when her peers injured or hurt themselves. When Hindley's father became disabled following a stroke, she would take her revenge for her mother and beat him. She called off her engagement with another man when she met Ian Brady and became obsessed with him even though he was frequently violent, and he drugged and raped her. She was submissive to his every demand and together they set out to murder children, hiding their bodies on the moor.

Neptune (Canto 13). Roman god of freshwater and the sea. His brother, Jupiter, was god of the heavens and the earthly world, and Pluto was god of the underworld. Neptune is often depicted as a tall, white-bearded man carrying a trident, a three-pronged fisherman's spear. He is also pictured with horses which drew the chariot he rode over the sea.

Like the oceans he ruled, Neptune had a tempestuous character, but he was also lascivious and enjoyed female conquests, both goddesses and mortals. He was attracted to the lovely maiden, Medusa, who was the only mortal of the three sisters known as the Gorgons. He proceeded to rape her in the temple of Athena, who was so outraged at the desecration of her temple, that she turned Medusa into a monster with the deadly capacity to turn anyone who looked at her to stone.

Nicholas III, Pope (Canto 30). He had been an honest cardinal but, as a pope, he indulged in large scale selling of objects belonging to the church (simony) in order to enrich himself and the Orsini family. He acquired significant wealth and a castle.

Through Pope Nicholas, Dante explains that souls can see into the future. Here in Hell, Nicholas mistakenly reveals the identity of both his successor, Pope Boniface VIII, who was still alive at the time Inferno was set, and even the next pope after that, Clement V, who was still alive at the time Inferno was written. Hell is a place where the past, present and future are blended together.

Nimrod (Canto 31). One of the giants in Hell and given a horn because, in the Bible, he was described as "a mighty hunter before the Lord".

Nimrod was the first king of Babylon and was responsible for the construction of the Tower of Babel which was designed to be high enough to reach Heaven. God was offended by the arrogance of the project and decided to confound the Babylonians' speech so that they could no longer understand each other by scattering them across the world. Mankind was once united by a universal language but, after Nimrod's offence, the world had to contend with a multiplicity of languages.

Osama bin Laden (Canto 14). Founder of the Islamic militant organisation, al-Qaeda, a designated terrorist group.

Widely thought to have been responsible for the 1988 bombings of the US embassies in Kenya and Tanzania, and the September 11th, 2001 attacks on the Pentagon and the World Trade Center. He was on the FBI's most wanted list for over ten years until his hiding place was located in Pakistan in 2011, when he was killed by US soldiers.

Passionfruit (Canto 15). Fictionalised former American Football running back, broadcaster and actor. He was charged with the murder of his former wife and her friend. While acquitted in a criminal trial, he was found liable in a civil trial and ordered to pay damages to the victims' families.

Phlegyas (Canto 8). Hell's ferryman who transports souls across the river Styx to Lower Hell where the sins of violence and fraud are punished. He is also guardian of the angry who are submerged in the river Styx.

RC-F2 (Canto 23). Fictionalised priest working at a Catholic primary school who got away with years of sexual abuse of young boys. He was eventually charged and imprisoned for paedophilia.

Tegghiaio Aldobrandi (Canto 15). Florentine Guelph nobleman. Spokesman of the Guelph nobles who advised against the disastrous expedition against Siena which ended in the defeat of the Florentines at Montaperti in 1260.

Tiberius, Emperor (Canto 23). 2nd Roman emperor ruling from 14-37 AD. He succeeded his stepfather, Augustus, and was a highly regarded military commander, receiving honours for his successes.

He had been obliged to divorce the love of his life, Vipsania Agrippina, when Augustus's daughter, Julia, became widowed. Augustus wanted Julia to be quickly and suitably married and he demanded that Tiberius fulfil that role. However, she was not faithful, and her acts of adultery pushed Tiberius away until he chose to exile himself on the island of Rhodes. There he indulged his sexual fantasies and became angry and resentful with nothing to do. Augustus did not let him return for almost ten years but when Tiberius's mother and Augustus' second wife, Livia, showed Augustus evidence of Julia's infidelity, he exiled Julia and, soon afterwards, he called Tiberius back to Rome. Augustus would have preferred to see one of Julia's sons become his heir, but one fell out of favour and the other two died in battle, leaving Tiberius as the only remaining choice to succeed him. Tiberius managed the imperial treasury well and his laws and policies were sensible. However, with the death of his son by Vipsania, Drusus, he took less interest in the running of the Empire and delegated his authority to Sejanus as chief administrator. He went to the island of Capri and never returned to Rome. He spent the last decade of his life a tyrannical recluse, inflicting terror on his subjects and killing anyone who was reported to him as having committed a crime even if the claim was unfounded. He indulged in perverted behaviour with young girls and boys encouraging fondling of his penis, group sex and anal sex, and was nicknamed "the old goat".

Tybalt Capulet (Canto 8). Juliet's cousin in William Shakespeare's tragedy *Romeo and Juliet*. He stokes the rivalry between his family, the Capulets, and the Montagues. He is loyal to his family, but he is fiery, impetuous and strong-willed.

When Romeo gate-crashes Lord Capulet's party in Verona, Tybalt's blood boils with anger and he longs to get back at Romeo for daring to mix with his family. Tybalt kills Romeo's friend, Mercutio, in what begins as a pretend duel, and Romeo avenges that death by killing Tybalt.

Tyler Durden (Canto 13). Protagonist in Chuck Palahniuk's 1996 novel *Fight Club*, which was adapted for film in 1999. Tyler Durden is the narrator's split personality and is born out of the narrator's insomnia-induced insanity and his disillusionment at the humdrum of society's norms.

Tyler Durden wants to bring the narrator to rock bottom so that he can resurrect himself, free from society's chains. The narrator starts to go to Fight Club which encourages men to beat each other up in bare-fisted fights. He starts to believe that violence is the vehicle for his powerless self to reassert himself against the corporate world he inhabits.

Ulysses (Canto 13). Greek hero who devised the strategy to capture Troy by smuggling in Greek soldiers hidden in the wooden horse. The taking of Troy led to Aeneas fleeing the city and subsequently founding Rome. Ulysses was also responsible for stealing the statue of Pallas on which the safety of Troy was believed to depend.

On his way from Troy to Ithaca, Ulysses was said to have been detained by the sorceress, Circe, on her island and she turned several of his company into swine.

Virgil (Canto 1). Virgil acts as Dante's guide through Hell and beyond into Purgatory.

His character stands for reason and, as a famous poet from the Classical era, he represents wisdom and virtue. What Virgil has achieved in his most famous work of literature, the Aeneid, *puts him at the height of ancient civilisation and the medieval Dante sees himself as taking on the mantel for "modern" literature.*

William and Maud de Braose (Canto 33). William married Maud in 1166 when she was just 11 and they lived under the rules of the English Kings Henry II, Richard I and John.

William earned the wrath of the Welsh when he committed the Abergavenny murders in 1175, tricking various Welsh princes and leaders to come to a conciliatory dinner only to have them murdered by his men. In 1199, William fought alongside Richard I at Châlus in France when the king was mortally wounded. He supported King John's claim to the throne and became a court favourite. John gave him land and castles, and it is thought that he may have tasked William with the murder of his nephew, Arthur of Britanny. However, William soon fell out of favour with the king who claimed he owed money from his estates to the Crown. King John used this to justify the seizure of William's estates across England and Wales.

Maud made no secret of the fact that she believed John had given instructions to murder Arthur and the pair of them were hunted down. William fled to Ireland and then to France disguised as a beggar to evade King John's capture. Maud, however, was not so lucky. She was imprisoned with their eldest son, William, in the dungeons at Corfe Castle in Dorset where they starved to death. The speed of the de Braoses' fall alarmed the barons who considered it a sign of the king's volatile temperament. Clause 39 of the Magna Carta, considered to be a precedent for trial by jury, was included in part due to the desire for protection against arbitrary decision-making like the punishments surrounding the de Braose family.

William Makepeace Thackeray (Canto 6). British author born in Calcutta, India in 1811. He died in London in 1863 at the age of fifty-two. He was best known for writing Vanity Fair, a novel based on the Napoleonic period in England. Thackeray's life was beset by ill health due to overindulging in food and he is represented as a glutton in the 3rd circle of *Hell Unearthed.*

Thackeray's father was an administrator in the East India Company, but he died when William, his only child, was four years old. William was sent to school in England and had a lonely and miserable childhood. He toyed with the law and painting, but when he came into his father's inheritance at the age of 21, he squandered it on gambling and bad investments. His wife became insane after the birth of their third child. He took solace in friends and travel and wrote numerous articles for magazines and newspapers alongside his novels.

Wolf of the High Street, the (Canto 27). Fictionalised character who was convicted of fraud for manipulating stocks by issuing false statements to ramp up their price before selling out at the inflated price to make a profit.

Yéle (Canto 32). Fictionalised charity leader who accepted millions of dollars of donations to repair the damage caused by the Haitian earthquake in 2010.

Funds were donated to rebuild houses, provide sanitation, electricity and drinking water but many charitable organisations failed to apply the funds as intended and large sums were lost to fraud. A number of charities appointed foreign 3rd party contractors who had no local knowledge, and projects suffered bureaucratic delays and embezzlement.